The Dragon Clan

The enigmatic Dragon Clan watches and records the history of Rokugan from its mountainous lands in the far north of the Empire. The Kami Togashi was known for his great foresight. He took no part in the Tournament of the Kami that decided who would rule as Emperor, for he knew before it began that Hantei would be victorious. The clan that Togashi founded seeks to emulate his wisdom and follow his teachings, and in doing so subtly guide the Empire toward the best path.

Unlike the other Kami, Togashi left no heirs. The Tattooed Order that bears his name is in many ways a family, yet it does not concern itself with lineages, bloodlines, and marriages. The Mirumoto family, warriors known for their unique twin-sword style of *niten*, handle much of the business of the clan, allowing the Togashi monks to focus on spiritual matters. The courtiers of the Kitsuki family are equally unusual among the samurai, both renowned and maligned for valuing physical evidence in determining the truth. The mystics of the Agasha family study the physical world as much as they revere the spirits that occupy it, combining alchemy with their shugenja prayers.

Clan Champion Togashi Yokuni guides the clan from the High House of Light, greatest and oldest of the order's monasteries, where he spends most of his time in seclusion. Uniquely, the members of the Togashi are both samurai and monks, holding a nebulous place in the Celestial Order. Yet for all their eccentricities, the Togashi are due the full respect of any samurai, and bear the same burden of responsibility.

To Terrance and Megs for introducing me to L5R, and to Kyle, Adrienne, Alyc, and Wendy, for a truly amazing campaign. 蝶 氏 八千代!

Cover illustration by Amélie Hutt.

Map illustration by Francesca Baerald.

Color insert artwork by Tiziano Baracchi, Joshua Cairós, Mauro Dal Bo, Kevin Zamir Goeke, Daria Khlebnikova, Pavel Kolomeyets, Polar Engine, Scott Wade.

ISBN: 978-1-63344-361-7
Printed in China.

Fantasy Flight Games
1995 West County Road B2
Roseville, MN 55113
USA

Find out more about Fantasy Flight Games
and our many exciting worlds at

www.FantasyFlightGames.com

A

Legend of the Five Rings

Novella

The Eternal Knot

By Marie Brennan

Fantasy Flight Games

Rokugan

HIGH HOUSE OF LIGHT

FUCHI MURA

Unicorn Lands

Dragon Lands

Phoenix Lands

Lion Lands

OTOSAN UCHI

Shinomen Forest

Scorpion Lands

Northern Crane Lands

Crab Lands

Southern Crane Lands

The Shadowlands

Islands of Silk and Spice

Chapter One

What do you remember?

Her breathing slows to a steady, unhurried pace, her stomach rising and falling, her shoulders relaxing and her spine lifting straight. It is familiar habit, after so many years of training—but this time, she knows, will be different.

What do you remember?

Three sensei, facing her with unreadable expressions. The novices joke that they represent the three sins: desire for success, fear of failure, and regret for ever having started down this path. They never say it where the monks can hear, but she suspects that joke was old a century ago, and has been passed down through the generations, just like the teachings of their order.

Three sensei, and an afternoon of grueling examination. The nature of the elements and their role in the world. The power of the *kami*, from the seven Kami who founded the Great Clans to the animating forces of mighty rivers and mountains to the little *mikokami* that make up the physical world. The mysteries of the Void, the state of nonbeing, and the Spirit Realms that shimmer around and through mortal existence like the refracted light of a crystal. The Fortunes: seven great, ten thousand small. The Tao of Shinsei. All the spiritual wisdom the three sensei can wring from her, and no certainty whether it is enough.

What do you remember?

Before that, Migasha-sensei's fist hammering into her ribs. Just barely keeping her feet as he tries to hook one of them out from under her, retreating farther than she should, and the slight bend in his mouth that says he notices the error. Wading back in, feinting a kick with one foot and then lashing out with the other; it doesn't connect, but the bend in his mouth goes away. Breath grating in and out of her lungs, sweat stinging her eyes as it soaks through the white band tied around her forehead.

And all the while, knowing this is only the start. Of course the trials begin with a test of fighting skill, so that novices go into the spiritual examination battered and exhausted.

If it were easy, it wouldn't be a trial.

What do you remember?

Years at the High House of Light, blurring and slipping together like overwatered ink. Learning *jūjutsu* from Sanaki-sensei, meditation from Ryōshō-sensei, theology from Shikkyo-sensei. Chores: chopping wood, carrying water, scrubbing the flagstones of the courtyards and the polished wooden floors of the halls. Raking leaves from the gardens and pouring tea for the senior monks. Hardship and resentment, serenity and satisfaction, and the constant song of the mountain wind, chill even in summer, sharper than a blade in winter.

What do you remember?

Seeing the thousand stairs for the first time, the impossible climb from the deep green of the valley below to the austere heights of the monastery above. The stories claim the High House of Light can only be found by those who are meant to be there: a person who seeks it without cause or merit might wander in the mountains for a hundred years and not come across the road even with a map to guide him, while one who thinks herself a hundred miles away might find herself at the base of its stairs—if that is her fate.

As a child of eight, she shivers at her own temerity, believing she is meant to reach the hidden monastery. And yet an unspoken certainty drives her, out of Phoenix lands, through the Great Wall of the North, away from her old life and into her new.

What do you remember?

Life with her mother. A market town at a confluence of roads, big enough to draw travelers, but not one of the famed cities of Rokugan—barely even famed within its own province. Aika braiding her hair, singing her songs, buying her sweets when they had a little money to spare. Giving her two sticks to care for, one longer, one shorter, both cut to a child's size, because someday—Aika assumes—she will inherit the two swords that ride at her mother's hip.

Until the day she sees an old monk, his left arm ending at the elbow but still corded with muscle and glorious with intricate tattoos.

What do you remember?

Back and back and back, through the whole of her life...and past it.

To what came before.

It is a rare thing, remembering a previous life. In Meido, the Realm of Waiting, the souls of the dead are washed clean of their memories before proceeding to their next life as decreed by Emma-Ō, the Fortune of Death. Only a few cling to any recollection, and even then it is only shreds.

But with time, training, skill, those shreds can be recovered.

Once *she* was the gnarled old *ise zumi* whose presence inspired a child to seek out the High House of Light. Once *she* was the sensei rapping young students across the shoulders with a stiff cane when they nodded off while meditating. She has raked these garden paths before, painted the walls of the dormitory with white lime, known the pines of the neighboring peak when they were not so tall.

How many lifetimes? She cannot say. Even now, with realization flooding her, she cannot summon the memories with perfect clarity. They remain fogged, like the valley below on a cold morning, when the sun first floods it with gold. She knows only that she has been an ise zumi before—that they learn to master the power of their intricate tattoos not only through a childhood spent training but through whole lifetimes. Taking that power into themselves, controlling it, refining it, until it flows through them like their own blood and breath.

What do you remember?

She remembers who she is, and who she was.

And she feels the power returning, dancing across her skin like lightning, striking into the marrow of her bones.

Mitsu entered the room silently, easing the door closed so he would not disturb Gaijutsu-sensei. It was courtesy more than practicality; he suspected the mountains could erupt in flame and ash and the blind old man would go on working without pause. But courtesy still mattered.

The room was small and plain—not the sort of place where one would expect to see momentous things happen. The wall panels displayed ink-wash paintings of the mountains in a minimalist style popular four hundred years earlier. Along the back wall stood a small shrine, at the center of which was a candle. Yanai knelt before it with her hands linked in a mudra, eyes half-lidded, gazing unblinking upon the flame.

But Mitsu knew from experience that Yanai wasn't seeing it, any more than she had heard him enter or felt Gaijutsu-sensei's hand on her skin. She had already passed the third trial of her *gempuku*, meditating under the guidance of Kōtai-sensei until she recovered the truth of herself. Now she had sunk into a deeper trance, one that would sustain her until the tattoo master's work was done.

Gaijutsu's hands seemed to see what their master's eyes could not. One of his apprentices held the ink for him; his silk-bound needles found the mouth of the tiny pot without hesitation or error, then returned to the line in progress. A second apprentice held the skin of Yanai's bare scalp taut with one hand and wiped with the other, mopping away the blood that beaded up where the needles stabbed over and over again.

The tattoo along Yanai's right arm was already complete. Storm clouds and a serpent wound in thick curls around her biceps, with right-angled bolts of lightning spiking down onto her forearm. Something related to fighting, Mitsu suspected; she'd done well against Migasha. He had thrashed her, of course—nobody expected a novice going through their gempuku to hold their own against the senior jūjutsu sensei. The test was in how well she stood up to it.

Combat, spiritual matters, recollection of past lives, and finally this: the process that transformed a novice into an ise zumi, a tattooed monk.

Gaijutsu-sensei worked in a tireless rhythm, dipping and stabbing, dipping and stabbing. The outline grew even as Mitsu watched, but its shape…that refused to cohere into something recognizable, no matter how he craned his neck. He wished he could approach and take a closer look, but even for a monk of his status, there were limits. The clan champion himself might hesitate to peer over the tattoo master's shoulder.

It was done sooner than he expected. Gaijutsu-sensei laid down his needles and did not pick them up again, and Mitsu realized the scalp mark was complete. An ordinary tattoo would be done in stages—first the outline, then the fill, giving the skin time to heal and the colors time to set before another layer was added— but Gaijutsu-sensei's needles were *nemuranai*. The awakened kami within them let him work without pause. If he was stopping now, it was because he was done. The storm-clouded serpent on her arm faded from bruise-dark to lightning blue, but the mark on her scalp would remain pure black.

The apprentices began clearing away their master's tools. None of them said anything, and Mitsu hadn't spoken, but that didn't mean anything where Gaijutsu-sensei was concerned. He spoke without hesitation as he wiped off his ink-stained hands. "Help me lay her out, Mitsu-kun."

Serving as novitiates in the High House of Light taught even the children of high-ranking samurai not to scorn chores. Mitsu had been born a peasant, and the habit of hard work hadn't gone away after he'd passed his gempuku. He slid one of the wall panels aside, took out a thin futon cushion, and laid it out on the mat before the candle. Then he took Yanai by the shoulders.

She went limp at his touch. Not meditating any longer, but unconscious. Her head lolled against his arm, giving him a good view of the entire symbol: an intricate knot of lines, crossing over and under each other in an abstract shape that made his vision swim the more he tried to make sense of it.

He laid her down and straightened her legs, then tucked a small buckwheat pillow under her neck, making sure it didn't press against the lines at the base of her skull. "What *is* this?" he asked Gaijutsu-sensei, now that there was no risk of disturbing anything. The Heavens themselves couldn't wake her now, not until she was done recovering. "I have never seen anything like it." Ise zumi tattoos were usually creatures like his own tiger and dragon and monkey, or sometimes natural images like bamboo and her storm clouds. Abstract forms like the knot of lines weren't unheard of, but they were rare.

And usually important.

Gaijutsu-sensei waved his apprentices out the door. They bowed and left, cradling their master's needles and inks in their hands. "It is what I saw."

Not with his blind eyes. He was the monastery's tattoo master not only because of his long years of experience, but because of his gift: the ability to see in visions what marks each ise zumi should bear. Mitsu had never quite dared to ask whether that gift came from one of Gaijutsu-sensei's own tattoos, which covered his body from neck to wrist to ankle, or whether he'd always had that gift—if, perhaps, that was the reason he'd come to the High House of Light in the first place.

"Of course, sensei," he said. "But…what does it *do*?"

The tattoo master shrugged and made his way to the door, one careful but confident step at a time. "That is for her to discover."

Chapter Two

*Y*anai woke to stiffness the likes of which she hadn't felt since her earliest days at the monastery, when the grueling combination of chores and jūjutsu practice left her feeling like every inch of flesh had been beaten with a stick.

An involuntary groan escaped her as she sat up. It was as if every muscle had locked tight for hours…and maybe they had. The specifics slipped through her fingers like smoke when she tried to grasp them, but one glimpse of her right arm was enough to tell her that she hadn't imagined the feeling of lightning arcing through her skin.

I passed.

The thought made her dizzy—or possibly that was the lack of food. Monks were no strangers to fasting, but her last meal had come the morning her gempuku began, and who knew how long ago that had been. In between, she'd fought Migasha-sensei, answered endless questions, remembered her past lives, and received the first of her tattoos. It was enough to make anyone ravenous.

A sudden rustling of robes made her twitch away, but it was only a boy coming to help steady her. A novice, perhaps halfway through his training—Hikkon, that was his name. She herself had sat a vigil like his, when Enshi had gone through her own gempuku.

"How long?" she asked.

Her voice rasped like grit under a sandal. Hikkon handed her a cup of water, which she downed in one gulp. He left her side long enough to pour her another, and this time he brought the jug back with him. While she drank, he said, "You have been asleep for a little over a day."

Since Gaijutsu-sensei had finished with her. She examined the tattoo on her right arm, not quite succeeding at repressing a smile. The storm-shrouded serpent was a little swollen to the touch, but not badly so. Once her skin finished healing, the image would be magnificent.

And her other tattoo…

The faint burning on her scalp guided her hand. Her questing fingers encountered stubble—a little over a day's worth; someone must have shaved her head again before Gaijustu-sensei went to work—and a pattern of swelling whose details she couldn't make out. It extended from the top of her forehead to the base of her skull.

"What is it?" she asked Hikkon, hiding her frustration. Even with a good mirror, she wouldn't be able to see the top of her own head, which meant she couldn't admire her second mark.

Desire might be one of the three sins, but it would take a more enlightened soul than hers not to want to appreciate this moment.

The boy shrugged. "I do not know. It is…like a knot of lines? It makes my eyes swim if I try to look at it too closely."

A knot of lines. Every ise zumi tattoo was unique; there were some patterns, certain motifs that tended to map to certain effects, but no two were exactly the same. She'd never heard of a knot-like tattoo, though.

I wonder what it does?

She made herself stop poking at it. The skin was tender, and exploration wasn't making it feel any better. "Do you have any food?"

The question was reflexive, and foolish. She'd stood the same vigil for Enshi; she knew perfectly well what came next, and it wasn't a meal. Hikkon bowed in apology. "My instructions are to take you to wash when you are ready, and to notify Hassuno-sama that you are awake."

Because her gempuku wasn't entirely complete. She'd passed the trials, received her tattoos…but there was one thing left to do.

She drank the last of her water and said, "I am ready now."

Age had rendered Hassuno into an elegant skeleton, her flesh drawn as tight over her bones as the thin soil of the peaks over the stone below, but anyone who thought that made her weak was a fool. Tattoos covered both arms, both legs, winding across her chest and back; even in the cold environment of the mountains, she wore only a breastband and a loincloth. The clan champion was the *daimyō* of the Togashi family, but Hassuno was the *iemoto* of the school, the head of the Tattooed Order and the inheritor of its traditions.

Yanai had scrubbed herself from head to foot, not excepting her newly marked skin. That had been a form of self-inflicted torture, making her yelp a few words she must have retrieved from a previous life, because they certainly weren't anything she'd learned at the monastery. No bath, though—not until her tattoos healed. It left her feeling just the tiniest bit grubby…or maybe that was just in comparison to Hassuno-sama's presence.

Or the room they were in. The iemoto received her in a grand chamber whose walls depicted key moments from the life of Togashi-no-Kami: the fall from Tengoku, the Tournament of the Kami, his encounter with the Little Teacher, Shinsei. Hassuno-sama sat on a raised dais of mats, while Yanai knelt on the polished floor some distance away. Behind her was an array of monks in silent rows, and it was odd to think that she had probably known every single one of them in a previous life. They weren't just welcoming her to their ranks; they were welcoming her *back*.

Hassuno-sama read the formal phrases from a scroll, making official what the tattoos had already made a reality. Then one of her clerks laid a blank scroll in front of Yanai, spreading it flat with two jade bars, and set a stone, an ink stick, a tiny dipper of water, and a brush at her side.

She ground and mixed the ink, not hesitating. She'd made her choice before her gempuku began, and her experiences during it had only reinforced her decision—as if she'd known, even before she knew, what being here meant.

With bold strokes of the brush, she wrote her new name—*Togashi Kazue*—using the characters for "one eternity."

The clerk carried the scroll to Hassuno-sama, taking care not to smudge the fresh ink. The iemoto looked it over and nodded in satisfaction. "Togashi Kazue-san," she said. "Welcome to the order. May you serve the Dragon Clan well."

When Kazue finally left the reception chamber, she found that most of the monks had dispersed, but one was still waiting outside.

"Mitsu-sensei," she said, bowing.

The movement proved to be a mistake. Her dizziness made her stumble forward a half step, barely catching herself short of colliding with him. Embarrassment heated her cheeks. Mitsu was highly respected among the ise zumi; to the novices, he was nothing short of a legend. Having risen from peasant origins to senior status within the order, he traveled the Empire as freely as the wind, doing good and getting into trouble all in the same breath. He bore far more than Kazue's mere pair of tattoos, marked from scalp to calf with Gaijutsu-sensei's art: a walking example of what they all aspired to become.

Kazue had met him before, but now it was different. Now she was a monk, not merely a novice. She should conduct herself better. "Forgive me, Mitsu-sensei."

"*Senpai* to you, now," he said. His smile made it a friendly reminder, not a rebuke. "You are a full monk, Kazue-san. And one desperately in need of food, I think. Come with me, and I will talk while you eat."

She followed him to the refectory. In the normal way of things only two meals were served each day, and only the sick got food out of schedule. But perhaps the monks on cooking duty had been warned that she had just passed her gempuku, because she found herself holding a tray with hot soup, vegetables, and several rice balls that proved to be stuffed with pickled plum.

Mitsu-sensei—no, Mitsu-senpai; he was a senior colleague to her now—sat with her at one of the long tables. "Congratulations," he said.

Kazue swallowed an overlarge bite in her haste to clear her mouth. "It's nothing, really. Everyone says the sensei don't tap you for your gempuku unless they think you're ready." Not that this did anything to calm the nerves beforehand.

"But people do still fail," Mitsu pointed out. "And even if they were sure you were ready, that just means you passed your 'real' test weeks ago. So take pride in your achievement."

The more food she ate, the hungrier she seemed to get. Kazue drank half her soup, then said, "What now?"

He tilted his chin toward her. "Do you know what those do?"

Her tattoos. Kazue moved her right arm, watching the marked skin shift over her muscles. "Not yet, no."

"Then that is what you do now. Find out. Not immediately, of course; you need to let them heal. A few days at least for the arm, and from personal experience, I recommend waiting two weeks before you try to shave your head again." He ran one hand over his scalp tattoo, grinning ruefully at what was obviously an unpleasant memory.

Two weeks of letting her hair grow. It would be the longest it had been since she arrived at the High House of Light, a wide-eyed child of eight. Long enough to interfere with the tattoo's power; they had to be uncovered for her to invoke them.

But the arm—that she could start on sooner.

"As my duties allow," Kazue promised.

But Mitsu shook his head. "That *is* your duty right now. You will need to move out of the novice dormitory, of course, and there will be a few other minor matters to take care of. But you should not do strenuous work or training for a little while. And until we know what your tattoos do, we cannot properly determine what *you* should do."

It sounded suspiciously like free time—a concept more alien to her than the gaijin lands on the other side of the mountains. "Just…poke at them and see what they do?"

"Poke at them, wave them around, concentrate hard, whatever seems like it might have an effect. Just try to do it someplace safe." Mitsu grinned again, tapping one finger against the magnificent dragon that covered his head. Kazue had seen him demonstrate its power, one bone-dry summer when a lightning strike caused a wildfire near the monastery. Mitsu had stood in the river and breathed his own flames onto the opposite bank, starting a counterfire that robbed the wild one of fuel and kept it from approaching too close.

She wondered if her own tattoo would send out bolts of lightning, and vowed to be nowhere near anything flammable when she tested that theory.

Her itching scalp reminded her of the unfamiliar figure inked there. "What if I cannot figure it out?"

"You will in time," Mitsu said, unconcerned. "It may take a while, but I have never heard of an ise zumi who went through their entire life with a tattoo they could not use."

"Have you ever heard of one like this before?" she asked, gesturing at her head.

Was it her imagination, or did his attention sharpen, like a hawk sighting prey? "No," Mitsu said, his voice still casual. "But let me know when you figure it out—I am very curious to know."

Chapter Three

The tattoos would take some time to heal. There were spiritual techniques that could hurry the process along, but Kazue hadn't mastered any of them—and even if she had, Chasetsu-sensei, the monastery's senior physician, advised against using them. "Your body's ki is in flux right now," she said. "Best not to unbalance things further. You will heal soon enough."

On Chasetsu's recommendation, Kazue began her explorations gingerly. She'd had enough of sitting still, and since neither of her tattoos were on her legs, she undertook walking meditations, pacing slow circuits around one of the smaller stone gardens, her steps timed to her breathing. She could feel the latent power of the ink, just beneath the surface of her skin, but its nature and purpose remained opaque.

When this failed to produce insights, she grew bolder. Mindful of Mitsu's cautionary words, she left the High House of Light, descending the thousand stairs to the forest below. Running along the paths there showed her that neither tattoo had done anything for her endurance or her speed, but it went some way toward making her feel more like herself, after several days of forced inactivity.

On a bare crag overlooking one of those paths, she sat for a time in meditation, focusing on the sense of power in her right arm. Then she opened her eyes and exhaled.

Her breath joined the mountain wind and was lost.

So much for lightning.

Kazue got up, settled into a firm jūjutsu stance, and punched skyward. No bolt issued from her hand. Faintly disappointed, she leapt from the crag; after all, the tattoo showed clouds, and some ise zumi acquired the ability to soar as lightly as a feather. But she hit the ground with all the usual force and rolled to soften the impact.

When she rose to her feet, she saw a cluster of novices coming along the path, bearing new loads of firewood for the monastery. Their leader bowed in greeting, but said nothing as they continued on their way.

At the High House of Light, monks leaping off high rocks was hardly an oddity. And she, Kazue, was counted among their number now.

Again, she reminded herself. But that didn't make it any less satisfying.

By the end of the first week the swelling on her arm had mostly vanished. Kazue flexed it experimentally, gently brushing away the skin that peeled up from where Gaijutsu-sensei had inked her.

Then she punched the nearest tree.

Something flowed down her arm and into the wood. But nothing happened, and it felt like the time, early in her training, when she'd lost her temper and charged full force at Adaki, one of the senior students. Even at the age of twelve, he was built like the Great Wall of the North; he just stood there and let her bounce off his chest. After that, he'd called her Little Bean.

Kazue studied her fist, then the tree. Then she went back to the High House of Light and found Adaki.

His name was Shunrei now, having passed his gempuku several years before, but he hadn't gotten any smaller. "Why not," he said, grinning, when he heard what favor Kazue wanted. "But let us go outside."

They went into the courtyard outside the jūjutsu dōjō. During the late afternoon it was nearly empty, with only a few monks passing back and forth. Short of leaving the monastery entirely, that was as private as they were likely to get, but Kazue didn't mind. In fact, she realized, part of her wanted an audience.

Chiding herself for that silly desire, she gathered herself again, remembering the feeling from before, attuning herself to the latent power in her arm. Then she set her feet and drove her fist at Shunrei's chest with all the force body and ink could muster.

He flew backward like an arrow shot from a bow, clear across the courtyard and into one of the beams supporting the walkway around the dōjō. Kazue winced, but Shunrei got to his feet with a roar of surprised laughter. "You've got the storm in you now, Little Bean!"

Not lightning, but something akin to it. With practice—not all of it aimed at Shunrei—she found she was able to deliver that power not just with her right fist but with her left as well. The effect was never again as strong as that first time, but when Kazue stopped for the day, glowing with pride and exertion, she found Mitsu watching her.

He acknowledged her efforts with a pleased nod. "I thought it might be related to fighting," he admitted as she approached.

Kazue thumbed sweat out of her eyebrows. "Why did you not tell me, senpai?"

"Because this is part of being an ise zumi." Mitsu tossed her a towel to dry off with. "Learning to find your own power."

It made her think of the third stage of her gempuku, the meditation to draw out her memory of past lives. Lowering her voice as they left the courtyard, Kazue said, "What about people who have just joined the order? All of us must have done this for the first time, once. How did we figure it out then?"

"Good question," he said, and seemed to mean it. "I do not remember my own first life in the order well enough to say. You?"

Kazue shook her head.

"Then it will remain a mystery for now. Tell me what you think of your tattoo."

He wasn't asking whether she liked it. The tests didn't end after one's gempuku; they continued onward, through not just this lifetime but all the ones to come. Kazue shook out her arm and said, "I think that, with practice, I will be able to channel its effect through kicks as well, and elbows and knees—any sort of blow. And it was stronger when I struck Shunrei for the first time, which makes me think I can learn to control how much force I deliver." *Maybe even enough to shatter a tree.*

Mitsu nodded. "Which is important, when you do not want to do too much harm. If you had hit someone other than Shunrei with that initial strike, it might have injured them badly. But his crab tattoo makes him resilient."

"He was like that before he got tattooed," Kazue muttered, causing Mitsu to laugh.

They were almost at the baths. Mitsu halted and faced her. "Practice with it for a while, and see what you can do. But in a week's time, I will expect you to shave your head, Kazue-san."

She ran her palm across the stubble, long enough now to have softened. The skin beneath was still tender, and itchy with healing.

Not as itchy as she felt in her spirit, though. The exhilaration of using the storm-serpent tattoo for the first time was already fading, leaving her even hungrier to discover what the other one did.

She doubted it had anything to do with punching and kicking.

Mitsu seemed to read her impatience, even though she did her best to hide it. "A week, Kazue-san. Master one before you tackle the other. Or at least acquire basic competence with it."

She bowed to hide her embarrassment. "Yes, senpai."

The week passed with painful slowness. Kazue practiced with the storm-serpent tattoo, intermittently succeeding at channeling its force through something other than a fist, but failing more often than not. She knew that was at least partly because her heart wasn't in it: she wanted to be experimenting with something else entirely.

When the week was up at last, she got Enshi, the monk whose gempuku she had once sat vigil for, to shave her scalp. Kazue could do it herself, but it was common for the novices and monks to assist each other in the baths, and Enshi could more easily spot the areas that were still inflamed and take extra care around them.

"Any idea what it does?" Enshi asked when she had wiped away the last of the soap and trimmed hair.

The same question, again and again. Not everyone asked it that openly, but Kazue knew every last monk in the High House of

Light wanted to know the answer. "This will be my first chance to test it," she said. "Mitsu-senpai said not to until it heals. Thank you for your help."

Back out into the woods she went. This time it was less because she feared harming someone, and more because she wanted to work away from curious eyes.

The sunlight fell like gold dust through the pines as Kazue stood and thought through her various options. She told herself she was being thorough, giving the matter due consideration rather than flinging herself forward blindly.

But that was a lie, and she was a samurai. Honesty was one of the virtues of Bushidō.

The truth was, she was a little afraid.

Afraid that she might not be able to figure it out—which ought to make her try harder, but instead she shrank back. Afraid that it meant she had some significant destiny in the order, and she might not be equal to it.

Afraid of what the strange, interlacing lines of the tattoo might do.

Fear was one of the three sins. Kazue ran her hand over her scalp, a gesture she hadn't repeated so frequently since her earliest days as a bald-headed novice. Then she made herself take a deep breath and begin.

She swam in a mountain stream and proved she was immune to neither cold nor drowning. The same was true of fire. She tried to speak to birds, deer, and fish, and got ordinary noises in return. She listened to the wind and heard nothing but its usual sigh; she peered into the distance and saw nothing more than her own eyes could perceive.

Racking her memories from both this life and previous ones, Kazue thought of more unusual possibilities. But she couldn't whisper messages to someone at a distance. She couldn't change her shape. She couldn't heal herself or anyone else, climb walls like a spider, or read the traces of memory from objects people had once held. With the permission of her superiors, she asked a visiting Agasha *shugenja* to pray over her, beseeching the kami to heighten her senses; she had a brief understanding of what it was like to be a wolf, "seeing" the world through an intricate map of scents, but afterward the shugenja said it had been neither easier nor more difficult to affect her.

"No," Mitsu said when Kazue asked him hesitantly whether she should try more extreme tests. "The ability to come back from the brink of death has never taken any form other than a phoenix, and what you have is nothing like any kind of bird."

"What about spirits, then?" Kazue said. "I remember hearing of a tattoo from centuries ago that let its bearer trap spirits. The form it took was not like what I have, but—"

"But their shapes are not always the same," Mitsu finished. "Good point."

Kazue's pleasure at the praise dimmed in the face of practical concerns. "I do not know how to test it, though. I could wander the mountains for a month without chancing across a suitable spirit for me to test that theory on."

She could tell by the sudden light in Mitsu's eyes that he'd had an idea. "In that case, you need a guide."

Chapter Four

Kazue knew old Myobai-sensei. A whole generation of monks did, because they'd seen him wandering by as they labored in the gardens, raking or watering or pruning. He was one of the caretakers of those gardens, but his eyesight had failed him enough that his duties were light. The story among the novices was that his fern tattoo let him sense the health and well-being of plants, so his job was simply to walk around and tell the other gardeners what needed tending.

Mitsu laughed when she told him that. "I imagine stranger tattoos have happened—in fact, I know they have—but no. The fern does something else entirely."

They found Myobai clipping a tiny maple bonsai, feeling it gently with his hands before selecting where to apply his shears. "Sensei," Mitsu said with a bow, "Kazue-san here needs to find a spirit."

The old monk did not stop his study of the bonsai, tracing the line of one branch with a fingertip. "A particular spirit?"

"Just one that is not too dangerous."

"There are none here," Myobai-sensei said. Then he turned to look at Kazue, and the delight in his expression made him look more like an eager boy than a wrinkled old monk. "But there might be in the forest. Young—er—"

"Kazue," she said, mystified.

"Young Kazue-san. Do you know how to get along in the wilderness?"

Mitsu gave her an encouraging nod when she glanced at him. "Yes," Kazue said. The uncertainty in her voice wasn't for the answer. She loved the mountains, and had spent no small amount of time studying the plants and animals found there, how to read the weather, and how to create shelter.

She simply had no idea why he was asking.

But Myobai-sensei gave the tiny maple one last pat on its crown and bounced to his feet like she'd just taken twenty years off his age. "How soon can we leave?"

It turned out that Myobai-sensei's work in the garden was as much a concession to his love of nature as any kind of duty. In his day he had roamed the Empire, but unlike Mitsu, who spent most of his time around people and half of that around peasants, Myobai-sensei's purpose had lain in the wild parts of Rokugan.

And that was because of his tattoo. The fern inked along his left forearm had nothing to do with plants; instead, it allowed him to sense the presence of spirits. "All kinds," he said when Kazue hesitantly asked. "When I was young I was not as perceptive, so I mostly only felt the bigger and more powerful things. But now, I can feel everything—even the mikokami that make up everything around us."

"How do you not become overwhelmed?" she asked, fascinated. "Feeling all of that?"

He shrugged. "How do you not become overwhelmed, hearing the air around you all the time? You learn to disregard it. Unless the wind is loud—and that is what a powerful spirit feels like for me. But I've learned to listen to the quieter whispers as well."

They had, with Mitsu's help, obtained permission to roam the valleys around the High House of Light in search of a spirit, so that Kazue might find out whether trapping them was her tattoo's purpose. With Myobai-sensei's failing eyesight, that seemed rather hazardous to her, but he blithely dismissed the risk. "The earth kami will warn me if I am about to step wrong," he said, which she suspected might be an exaggeration. Mitsu had made it clear before they left that she was supposed to look after the old man.

At least he was still hale enough. He made no complaint about camping with only a tarp to cover them, even though the air still held a spring chill. And he regaled her with stories as they walked, describing all the spirits he'd encountered in his travels: everything from the powerful kami of an ancient oak to a graceful *tsuru* shapeshifter to a vengeful *onryō*, a ghost that had tried to kill him. "Even a *dodomeki* once," he said. "She was a human bandit who had turned into a *yōkai* because of her greed. Had bird eyes all over her arms. Much more difficult to sense, yōkai of that sort—the ones who started out human."

"What did you do when you found those things?"

He shrugged. "Pacified the ones who needed it, banished the ones who needed *that*. Had conversations with a few, but most of them are not much for talk. They either attack you or make strange noises that do not mean much to a human."

Their goal out in the wilderness was to find something relatively safe. "There is not likely to be anything dangerous nearby," Myobai-sensei said when they stopped to drink from a snowmelt stream. "Not much will venture this close to the monastery. I know a tree that is home to a *kodama*, but I do not want to disturb it; our best chance is to find some animal spirit for you to try."

True to his prediction, the first thing they stumbled across was a rabbit spirit. Or rather, Myobai-sensei's head came up and he sniffed at the air, then declared there was a rabbit spirit nearby. On his recommendation, Kazue built a free-running snare, which would catch but not harm whatever wandered into it. Then she set it along a rabbit trail with a small pile of clover as a combination of offering and bait, and they waited.

And waited, and waited. "It may take a while," Myobai-sensei said cheerfully.

Kazue settled into the lotus position and began to pray, asking the rabbit spirit to assist her in her attempt to learn the nature of her tattoo.

Either the spirit didn't hear her, or it didn't feel cooperative. It took several more days and Myobai-sensei alerting her to a monkey spirit, an otter spirit, and another rabbit—or possibly the same one—before they located a *kappa* in one of the mountain streams. Kazue, watching it from hiding, focused on the tattoo on her scalp and tried to direct its power at the turtle-like creature, but nothing happened.

"That is yours to decide," Myobai-sensei said when she asked him what she should do.

It didn't seem right to kill the kappa. They could be malevolent, but most of the time their mischief was harmless. Dredging through her memories from this life and those before, Kazue went out and bowed to the kappa, forcing it to respond with the same gesture, spilling the water from the dish in its head. With the kappa thus weakened, she made it promise not to drown or otherwise harm any human beings.

When that was done, Myobai-sensei said, "Well, it *is* a yōkai. Possibly you need a proper spirit, something like a ghost."

"I don't think so," Kazue said, discouraged. "It felt…like I was trying to point with an arm I don't have at something that was not there. If this was meant to work on spirits, I think I would have felt more than that. Or maybe I'm wrong?" She slapped her thigh in frustration. "What do I know."

"More than anyone else does," he said gently. "Trust your instincts, Kazue-san. You are the only one who can say what you do or do not feel from your tattoo."

His words made her go still, thinking. "Maybe not the only one," she murmured. "What about Gaijutsu-sensei?" He was the one who had seen it in a vision and inked it into her skin. If anyone could give her insight, he could.

But Myobai-sensei shook his head. "I can tell you right now what he will say if you ask. 'That is yours to discover.'"

Much like Mitsu's advice not to shave her head too soon, it had the ring of personal experience. "How long did it take you to learn the use of your tattoo?" Kazue asked, nodding at the fern on his arm.

He patted the mark like an old friend. "Not long. But that is because an Isawa shugenja came to the monastery with the *bakeneko* she kept as a pet."

Trust an Isawa to keep a demon cat as a pet. Kazue squared her shoulders and said, "I know you would be happy to stay out here longer, Myobai-sensei, but I should return to the monastery."

He sighed in resignation, but nodded. "Follow your path, Kazue-san. The Fortunes will bring you to understanding when it is time."

Chapter Five

"Enshi-san," Kazue said, "could I ask a favor of you? It is very odd to me that everyone else can see what is tattooed on my head, but I cannot."

"You still do not know what it does?" Enshi said sympathetically. "I do not know if seeing the shape of it will make anything clearer, but let me get my brush."

The monks of the High House of Light weren't renowned for any art form other than tattooing, but their order didn't discourage them from pursuing activities that might help their spiritual development. Enshi was a reasonably accomplished painter, and Kazue expected the process of sketching her tattoo would be a quick one.

After Enshi had thrown away three attempts, though, Kazue realized it wouldn't be so easy. "I am sorry. If I had known it would be this much trouble, I would not have bothered you. Do not inconvenience yourself any more, please."

"Stay right where you are," Enshi said, laying out another scrap of paper. "I do not know why this is so difficult—it is not as if the lines are moving. But I will get it right if it takes me all day. They say challenges are good for spiritual growth."

It didn't take quite all day, but they nearly missed the evening meal. Enshi's determination rewarded Kazue with a small, intricate painting, allowing her to see at last what Gaijutsu-sensei had inked into her scalp.

She felt none of the strange effects other people had described, but that wasn't surprising. The figure itself was not, she thought, in any way significant: it reminded her a little bit of one of the mandala scrolls given as a gift to a previous Dragon Clan Champion and now hanging in the eastern meditation hall, but apart from that it resembled nothing Kazue had seen before. Whatever sensation people got upon trying to study it closely must come from the tattoo itself, not the shape it took.

But its abstraction reinforced her feeling that the tattoo's unknown effect wasn't something material. It wouldn't make her stronger or faster, wouldn't allow her to perform physical feats beyond the human norm. Its power was more subtle than that, and to find it, she must look inward.

So she returned to meditating. The next morning, she didn't join her fellow monks for the meal; she went instead to the eastern meditation hall, where she seated herself in front of the mandala scroll and focused her mind on its intricate figure. This hall was less often used because its floor needed replacing; here she would be undisturbed.

Kazue sat in a trance for hours. She knew already that the tattoo hadn't removed her need for food or water—she still got hungry and thirsty, just like before—but clearly she couldn't expect it to unfold its secrets with a few minutes' effort. She was determined to undertake a fasting meditation for at least three days before she gave up.

It didn't take that long.

Near sunset, she began to grow restless. Her mind, which had rested with perfect serenity on the mandala for most of the day, rippled with a nebulous and distracting sensation. Rather than fighting it, Kazue shifted her focus to that sensation, allowing it to become the object of her meditation. *What am I feeling?*

Gradually she realized the ripple originated from outside her own mind. Rising, Kazue formed one hand into a fist and covered it with the other in a meditative mudra, then began walking, as she had done before. Her steps were slow and perfectly balanced, three per breath. With her eyes half-closed and downcast, she moved toward the door of the meditation hall, out onto its veranda, into her sandals, and then down and around the corner into one of the gardens.

This garden was even less used than the hall. It lay in the shadow of a high wall and received very little sunlight; most things planted there died, and so it had been transformed into a rock garden not long after Kazue first came to the monastery. But no one had wanted to remove the enormous pine tree that grew in one corner, so the monk in charge of the transformation had attempted to design around it. The results were less than successful, and since then the pine had reigned over a forgotten expanse of gravel and small boulders.

The branches of the tree drooped nearly to the ground, despite the wooden crutches propping them up. Kazue's instinct led her toward it. When she knelt, the sensation vanished, and she saw that someone was hiding under the branches.

A boy, dressed in novice robes, and no more than nine or ten years old. His expression was more guilt than anything else—clearly he wasn't where he should be, and now a monk had caught him shirking—but his posture, curled tight with his arms around his knees, and the marks still streaking his face, told Kazue that guilt wasn't the main thing on the child's mind.

She offered him a smile, unsure whether he could see it in the dim light. "What is your name?"

"Saburō," he said. Then he flinched. "Kanta."

New enough to the monastery that he wasn't used to his novice name. Saburō—that meant he was someone's third son. Unusual in Dragon lands these days; even in a monastery, surrounded by celibate monks, Kazue had heard about the infertility plaguing the people of the Dragon Clan. It must have gone hard with this boy's parents, if they were Dragon: seeing the Fortunes bestow such a blessing, then losing the child to a life among the ise zumi.

It was an honor, having one's child join the order. But even for dutiful samurai, honor of that sort could be difficult to bear.

The boy shamed himself, crying in a corner like this. But Kazue had done much the same when she first came to the monastery, as had many of her fellow novices—though her hiding spot had been behind a tall boulder in the southern garden. Other children grew up knowing they might follow in the footsteps of one of their parents, training as a *bushi* or courtier or shugenja, but ise zumi almost never had families of their own; everyone who arrived at the High House of Light came here a complete stranger, unfamiliar with anything more than legends. Even if they had sought it out of their own free will, the change went hard, and it would be many long years of training before most of them realized they had been here before.

She couldn't tell Kanta that. It was a secret revealed only during the gempuku, and then only to those who proved their readiness.

But she could try to ease his way. "I am Kazue," she said. "It does get easier, Kanta. I know that may be hard to believe now, and there will be times you will wish you had never set out for the High House of Light…but you would not have made your way here if you were not strong. The weak never find this place."

The light was fading fast. She could just make out Kanta's jaw tightening as he failed to hold back a wet sniffle. "Genzeki says it's weak to cry."

Not a name Kazue recognized; she assumed that was another novice. "Courage lies in knowing fear, and overcoming it; strength lies in knowing weakness, and getting up again. You will get up again. And when you do, you will understand strength better than Genzeki does."

Kanta shifted. "They'll beat me for running away."

Kazue held out one hand, palm up. "Yes. But that will only hurt your flesh. Separate yourself from it; learn to experience pain from outside. Then it will no longer rule you."

She knew her words weren't precisely comforting. Anything else would be dishonest, though—she and Kanta both knew the punishment he faced. The best help she could give him was instruction in the proper way to bear it.

He accepted her hand, and she drew him out from under the tree. "If you hurry," Kazue said, "you can return to the dormitory before dark." The consequences would get more severe after that.

Kanta started to run, stopped, flung an awkward bow at her, and took off again.

Alone in the pine garden, Kazue ran her hand over her scalp. A faint smile rose to her lips.

The tattoo had guided her.

Not in what she had said to Kanta. That had been all her own doing; she'd lost the tenuous thread of connection to her tattoo when she saw him under the tree. But it had alerted her to his presence.

Other monks could sense living creatures around them. She didn't know of any who could sense the distress of those creatures.

No wonder I had so much trouble figuring it out. This is a monastery; we're supposed to be serene.

Smoothing her own expression into serenity, if not her heart, Kazue went to find Mitsu.

Chapter Six

"Distress." Mitsu tapped one finger against his knee, thinking.

Kazue couldn't tell what he thought of her tale. Her satisfaction over having figured out her tattoo's effect had faded while she described it; what had seemed in the moment like a great victory had grown smaller in the telling. When strange or unique tattoos appeared, it usually heralded some kind of destiny within the order. But what destiny could be linked to sensing the presence of emotional conflict?

She was glad they were talking privately, in one of the rooms used for individual instruction. Kazue had made herself wait until after the evening meal, because even when her discovery seemed momentous, it wasn't worth disrupting the monastery's routine. Mitsu must have seen the excitement in her bearing, though, because he had approached her as soon as the meal was done and led her to this room to talk.

His finger stilled. "Call on the tattoo now," Mitsu said. "Tell me if you sense anything. I want to see how far it reaches."

Kanta had been very nearby—just on the other side of the wall from where Kazue had sat in meditation. But just as her storm-serpent tattoo could be used to varying degrees, she might be able to get more from the knot. Kazue drew in a breath and exhaled it slowly, closing her eyes, attuning herself to the lines inked into her scalp.

Nothing. However far the effect extended, it seemed there was no one within range who felt distress.

"I am sorry, senpai," Kazue said. "I do not think it goes very far—at least not yet."

When she opened her eyes, a tear was slipping down Mitsu's cheek.

He wiped it away with a deliberate hand. "I do not think it is emotional distress that you sense, Kazue-san. Something similar, perhaps—but if that were it, you would have sensed me."

Startled, she said, "But you're one of the most—"

She stopped herself before she could finish the sentence, but Mitsu nodded anyway. "One of the most advanced monks in the order. Yes. But although I have learned to cultivate serenity, that does not mean I lack the capacity to feel."

"What were you thinking about?"

The question was beyond impertinent. Kazue realized, too late, what had troubled her about the tattoo's effect—or rather, its supposed effect. If she could sense other people's distress, then its function was to undermine their *tatemae*, their outward mask of composure. Though it might serve a useful purpose, it also shamed the target, exposing their true feelings despite their best efforts to keep those honorably concealed.

"Forgive me, Mitsu-senpai," she said, bowing to the floor. "I should not have asked."

"It is nothing, Kazue-san." She straightened in time to see him smile sadly. "Unlike most in our order, I have traveled the Empire from one end to the other. We are samurai as well as monks, and both codes teach us the importance of compassion. I have seen enough suffering to make any compassionate heart weep."

Kazue's cheeks heated. "Yes, senpai." Even if the tattoo didn't actually undermine tatemae, she had succeeded in making Mitsu reveal more than he should have.

His finger went back to tapping against his knee as he thought. "Not distress, then, but something else. That which is hidden?

No—if it were that, you would have figured it out long before now. Something rarer, then. Something more subtle."

Then he cocked his head to one side. "You have thought of something, Kazue-san."

"No," she said, shoulders tensing. "Not exactly. That is…"

He leaned forward. "Do not be reluctant to say it. This is quite a puzzle; any clue might be of use."

She dug her own fingers into her knees. "I think…just as the storm-cloud serpent can be used to greater or lesser degree, I think this one has more purpose than merely to sense—whatever it is I sensed. That is only the smallest part of what it does. I feel as if…as if there is a way for me to use it in a more directed fashion."

"Directed. You mean *on* someone."

She could read his thoughts as if a scroll had unrolled over his face. Sudden apprehension drove her next words out in a hurry. "Mitsu-senpai—I think it might be dangerous."

He eased back, not retreating, but considering. "How so?"

"I do not know," Kazue admitted. She would have preferred to leave this unspoken; it was all guesswork, vague fumblings toward an understanding of something she had only used once, and imperfectly at that. "Just that when I imagine trying to focus its power on someone, I feel like I am standing at the edge of a cliff. Or like *that* person is. And it would be irresponsible of me to push them over the edge without knowing what is at the bottom."

She phrased it in suitably sensible, dutiful terms. Calling the idea "irresponsible" was better than admitting what she really felt: fear.

When she thought about unleashing the tattoo on someone—not merely sensing something from them, but directing its power against them—what she felt then wasn't a cliff. It was a canyon. A crevasse leading downward into darkness. Ise zumi like Shunrei were trained to withstand all kinds of physical blows, but who would be able to resist this?

She had no way of knowing, because she didn't even know what *this* was. But one thing was certain: she wasn't going to try it out for the first time on one of the most respected monks in the order.

Given Mitsu's reputation for impulsive action, she almost expected him to insist on trying anyway. But he didn't command such respect simply for his ability to punch things; he nodded his agreement, and she tried not to sag in relief. "Leave it alone for now," he said. "I will consider what the next step should be. In the meanwhile, I think it is time you assumed your normal duties. Talk to Rōju-san and he will make the arrangements."

She bowed in obedience as Mitsu climbed to his feet. Embarrassment and gratitude warred in her heart. *I should have been able to figure this out by now. But at the same time…I'm glad not to keep pushing at it.*

If that was weakness, then she would have to remember the advice she'd given Kanta—and get back up again.

Mitsu had expected it would take longer to receive an audience with the clan champion.

Like all of his predecessors, Togashi Yokuni was reclusive. Whereas most clan champions lived in palaces at the hearts of major cities in their realms, surrounded by all the bustle of government and trade and art, the leader of the Dragon lived at the High House of Light, in a remote set of chambers connected to the rest of the monastery by only a single gate. He rarely appeared among the ise zumi, and he conducted most of his duties via messengers. A simple monk like Mitsu, however advanced, might wait for weeks or months before getting the opportunity to speak with him.

Instead, Mitsu was summoned the next day.

The degree of speed was surprising, but not the fact of it. Mitsu had suspected for some time now that he was being considered for some particular duty. After years of wandering the Empire without restraint, he'd come back to the High House of Light only to find Hassuno-sama ordering him to stay for a time. Then he was assigned to oversee Kazue after her gempuku—a task that had proven more complex than he anticipated.

Perhaps the clan champion had foreseen what was coming with Kazue. The legends said Togashi's heirs were blessed with a degree of his foresight. Who could say where their vision would guide them?

Mitsu climbed the narrow steps that led to the audience chamber. Anywhere else in the Empire it would have been a broad staircase, flanked by statues and banners, but the Champions of the Dragon were chosen from the ranks of the ise zumi. While they lived in more splendor than the average monk, it was still ascetic by the standards of the other clans.

Two guards stood outside the chamber. One was a bushi of the Mirumoto family, armed and armored; the other was one of Mitsu's own senpai, a woman covered with tattoos for striking and defending, as well as for sensing possible threats.

They opened the doors for him, and he entered the presence of Togashi Yokuni.

Like the entrance outside, the chamber was austere, expressing its beauty through simplicity rather than opulence. The grain of the polished wooden floor shone gold in the light from the lamps, and the lamps themselves, though gilt, were elegantly spare. The wall panels changed with the seasons; now, in the trailing end of spring, they showed wisteria blossoms, with swallows flitting among them. The hangings around the dais were antique silk and matched the delicate shade of the wisteria.

Amid this elegance, the Dragon Clan Champion stood out like a mountain peak. Although he came from the ise zumi, he wore armor from head to foot, including a *mempō* that completely obscured his face. It should have meant he could not call on any of his tattoos, but Mitsu took it for granted that the armor was a nemuranai. Its awakened spirit might bestow all kinds of benefits on the wearer.

But it meant that the champion was reclusive even in person, his body and face entirely hidden from view. The samurai who acted as his body servants were the only ones who had seen Yokuni unmasked since his accession, and their discretion was as steadfast as stone.

Mitsu bowed to the floor. "You honor this unworthy one, Togashi-ue."

"Rise, and speak."

Had all of Yokuni's predecessors been as terse as he was? The ise zumi cultivated many talents, but flowery rhetoric was rarely one of them. Mitsu had seen Crane courtiers in their domains; it could take them a quarter of an hour to get to the point. Here it was always brief.

Mitsu described Kazue's experience with Kanta, and the discussion that followed. "Unless she tests her tattoo's power on a subject," he said, "she will have no way of understanding its full effect. But since this may endanger the target, I feel that it should be used on someone possessed of great physical, mental, and spiritual strength, who might be able to withstand its force. Togashi-ue, I request permission to offer myself as that subject."

He'd almost said it the night before, when the idea first came to him. But although samurai weren't supposed to fear death, there was a very large difference between not fearing it and courting it recklessly. Like all his kind, Mitsu owed a duty to his lord, and that duty included not scrambling his mind like an egg without obtaining permission first.

"No," the clan champion said.

Mitsu had enough self-control not to rock back in surprise. *I was so sure…*

Why else would Hassuno have told him to stay, then assigned him to Kazue, if not for this? She had some purpose in mind for him, likely received from Yokuni; was it not to help Kazue discover the nature of her new power? When he was summoned so promptly to this audience, Mitsu had thought his suspicions confirmed.

"Togashi-ue—" he began, even though arguing was a breach of etiquette in this court as in any other.

"That is not your path," the clan champion said. "Nor is it hers. The tattoo Kazue-san received will show its true power in due course—but you must find some other for her to use it on."

Silence fell. Mitsu waited three heartbeats, to see if there would be anything more; in addition to being terse, Yokuni also paused for thought. But the clan champion said nothing else, and so Mitsu bowed again. "I understand, Togashi-ue."

It was both true and not. He didn't know where he was supposed to find a suitable target for Kazue—or what a suitable target would even look like.

But he did understand that finding the answer to that was a test for him as well.

Chapter Seven

No one spoke about it openly, but within a day Kazue was sure that every ise zumi at the High House of Light knew she had failed.

I haven't failed, she told herself. *It's only been a few weeks. No one has seen anything like this before; it's reasonable that I might need more time to figure it out.*

Reasonable, yes. But she still felt the collective breath the monastery had held, and the collective exhale of disappointment when they resigned themselves to not learning the answer any time soon.

She hadn't gone through years of training for nothing, though. Ise zumi, like all monks, like all samurai, were supposed to bear hardship with stoicism. Kazue walked through the series of three gates in the northeastern corner of the complex, symbolically stripping herself of desire, fear, and most of all, regret. Then she lit incense and prayed for wisdom, and when that was done, she applied herself to her duties.

Which for now consisted of working in the scriptorium, writing out copies of texts that had been requested by samurai elsewhere in Dragon lands, or even farther away. The library of the

High House of Light was far from the most impressive in Rokugan, dwarfed by the archives of the Ikoma and the Phoenix, but it held a great many esoteric writings, including an assortment of legends and fables from which grains of truth might fall. The courtiers of the Dragon traded copies of those materials for political favors from scholarly monks, courtiers, and shugenja.

The work was straightforward and meticulous. It also locked her away from sunlight and fresh air—but that was a small price to pay for also being sheltered from the view of others. In the scriptorium, she could pretend that no one was waiting for anything at all. Here she didn't feel like a scroll was dangling around her neck, labeling her as *Togashi Kazue, the monk who can't use her tattoo.*

As the days went by, though, that shelter started to feel more and more like a hiding spot. Like she was Kanta, huddling under the tree. If she'd still been a novice, she would gladly have come out and taken her punishment, if it meant she could have a sensei tell her what to do. But she was a monk, and the lesson here was one nobody else could teach her.

Mitsu found her there a month later. Kazue almost botched the character she was writing, she was so surprised to see him. She didn't think he'd forgotten her, not exactly…but she'd convinced herself that "I will consider what the next step should be" had been a polite way of telling her to solve the puzzle on her own, and that the time elapsed since then was just more evidence of her failure.

She'd tried. And Mitsu clearly knew that, or at least guessed, because the first thing he said to her was, "How much dust did you get on yourself, digging out old records of strange tattoos past?"

"Very little," Kazue said with dignity. "The caretakers of the library are much too diligent to let dust gather."

"Did you find anything useful?" He shook his head before she could answer. "No, of course not, or you would have told me."

It wasn't quite true. She'd found accounts of ise zumi past who took far more than a few months to learn the purpose of their tattoos, because the effects weren't amenable to being revealed through ordinary experimentation. One man had spent decades at the High House of Light without ever knowing the purpose of the humble catfish tattoo on his right leg, until the day a catastrophic earthquake shook the mountains. He had slammed his feet down like a *sumai* wrestler and the ground beneath the monastery fell still, while the slopes all around them crashed down in landslides.

I just hope it won't take me fifty years to learn what this knot does. Impatience was a form of desire, but surely it wasn't too much to ask that she be able to use her tattoo sooner than half a century from now.

She said, "Do you need me for something, Mitsu-senpai?"

"Finish your work today," he said, "but tomorrow, someone else will have to take on that duty for you. We leave at dawn."

It was a good thing she had laid her brush down, or she would have dropped it. "Leave?" Her heart thudded. *They can't be casting me out.*

A foolish thought. "Fuchi Mura," Mitsu said. "I have arranged a way for you to test your tattoo. Whether it will be useful, who can say—but at least we can try."

Fuchi Mura. Was that one of the villages she'd passed through on her way to the High House of Light as a child? She couldn't remember, and hadn't left the monastery since. Short journeys into the surrounding wilderness for her training or tattoo experiments didn't count. The rest of Dragon lands—much less the rest of the Empire—had come to seem almost imaginary to her, like a story made up by visitors to entertain the monks.

More foolish thoughts. Kazue hoped neither her sudden excitement nor its accompanying apprehension had shown through. "Of course, senpai. Is there anything I should prepare?"

He studied her critically. "You have probably never been on a horse."

"My mother could not afford one, senpai. A bushi did take me on a ride once, though, during a festival."

"So in essence, no." He considered it, then shook his head in humorous resignation. "Mortification of the flesh has its spiritual merits, but I do not want saddle sores distracting you when we arrive in Fuchi Mura. It is only a few days away; we will walk."

Summer had arrived in the Great Wall of the North. The peaks retained their caps of snow, but even the most sheltered valleys below were green and lush. The passes took them up through stony regions carpeted with mountain heath, then lowered them into dells of false hellebore and sturdy rowans, which the monks often cut for firewood. The cherry trees had long since shed their blossoms, but the rowans were studded with bursts of white.

Kazue breathed the air in deeply, tilting her face to the sun. She wasn't aware of Mitsu watching her until he said, "You enjoy being out here."

"I am happy at the monastery," she said hurriedly, composing herself once more.

"I did not suggest otherwise. But copying texts is the wrong duty for you, I think. Your calligraphy is good enough, and you seem to be diligent, but sealed away in the scriptorium is not where you belong."

They were traveling alone. Kazue remembered high-ranking samurai passing through the town where she grew up, accompanied by grand entourages: *jizamurai* vassals, peasant *ashigaru*, servants, whole caravans of people to assist them. The visitors to the High House of Light were usually much less ostentatious, but whether that was because the Dragon were a relatively poor clan or because they knew no one at the monastery would be impressed by displays of power and wealth, Kazue didn't know. Mostly their retinues consisted of armed escorts, because there were bandits in the mountains.

She pitied whatever bandits thought it a good idea to attack two lone monks. Mitsu on his own could probably rout an entire gang, and she wouldn't mind the chance to call on the one tattoo whose use she knew. But bandits were generally smart enough to avoid *ise zumi*, because they never knew what strange abilities they might face.

All the monks knew Mitsu was being considered for some kind of elevation or special duty. His own words had confirmed it, in a roundabout way: he had spoken as if he had the power, or at least the influence, to have her reassigned from the scriptorium. His frequent absences from the monastery meant he held no official title there, but if Kazue were asked to list the most important monks in the order, his name would be among them. Yet he was out here with her, walking along a narrow mountain trail, with no one to accompany them.

Then again, he usually traveled alone. She was already more escort than he was accustomed to.

"If you think that would be best, senpai," she said. "I am happy to serve wherever I can best be of use."

"A properly dutiful answer," Mitsu said. "But ours is a strange situation, Kazue-san. Like all samurai, ise zumi are expected to do as our lord commands, regardless of personal desire. But you have passed your gempuku; you know that you have been in the order before. What do you recall from that?"

Of specifics, very little. She knew Mitsu wasn't asking for the names she'd borne, though, or the deeds she'd performed. "We reincarnate into the order to hone our spiritual power across multiple lifetimes."

"Yes. Our discipline is not that of Brotherhood monks, whether they propitiate the Fortunes or seek Enlightenment through the Tao of Shinsei. We cultivate ourselves to better serve the Dragon Clan and its champion."

"And sometimes," Kazue said slowly, "cultivating ourselves takes us down...unusual paths."

Her restrained choice of words made him grin. "You must have remembered at least one lifetime when you went out into the world. You know our reputation."

For most Rokugani, the ise zumi were a colorful legend, as exotic as the yōkai that haunted the wilderness and far less predictable. Kazue hadn't attended a single play in this lifetime, but she knew that tattooed monks were a stock figure in certain kinds of stories, appearing out of nowhere to do something inexplicable that inevitably turned out to be important.

"We have more freedom," she said. "More opportunity to do whatever seems right or necessary."

"And at the same time, we have *less*," Mitsu said. "Because while we pursue our individual growth, we do so in the service of a single purpose—not only in this lifetime, but in many to come."

The paradox felt comfortable, like a well-worn pair of sandals. Kazue hesitated, wondering if she should speak her mind. The question that haunted her had been with her through more than one lifetime, and she'd never answered it to her satisfaction.

If there was anyone she could ask, though—anyone who might be able to answer—it was Mitsu.

"But what is that purpose?" she said. "Each of us spends most of our lifetimes in the High House of Light, meditating, training, strengthening ourselves—but then not employing that strength. There are monks with tattoos for attack and defense who will die without ever using them against an enemy. Some lifetimes we go out into the world, and then our abilities may make a difference… but those lives are rare. Why did Togashi-no-Kami establish the order, then instruct us to keep ourselves so much apart?"

Mitsu locked his hands behind his back, across the tail of the tiger that crouched in his skin. "Perhaps for those occasions when we *do* go out. The power we have is difficult to master; maybe all the lifetimes of seclusion are necessary preparation for those few moments when we make a difference."

That was one of the tenets of their order: to find the balance between contemplation and action. Learning to recognize the right moment to tip fate in one direction or another.

But Kazue, studying the line of Mitsu's shoulders, didn't believe that was all.

"You think there is more to it," she said softly.

He bent to dig a pebble out of his sandal, and for a moment she thought he wouldn't answer. When he straightened up, though, his smile was rueful. "I suspect so, yes. But it is a suspicion only."

"Togashi-no-Kami was famed for his foresight," she said. "If anyone would have established an order of monks, drawn back again and again through the cycle of reincarnation, honing their power for some decisive moment far in the future…it would be him."

"But what moment?" Mitsu said, finishing her thought. "I do not know, Kazue-san. Whatever it is, it may not come in this lifetime, or the next."

They were ise zumi. A thousand years from now, they would still be here—or rather, be here again—ready to serve the Dragon and the Empire.

Mitsu nodded at Kazue, and she realized he was indicating the tattoo on her scalp. "Something like that does not come at random. I think you have it because of your efforts in previous lives, because you have cultivated yourself to the point where you can bear whatever that is. So while caution is good, Kazue-san…do not fear your own power."

She resisted the urge to duck her chin. "I will do my best, Mitsu-senpai."

He started walking again, and she hurried to catch up. Over his shoulder, he said, "And I will suggest you be removed from duty in the scriptorium. I do not know what your fate is in this lifetime, Kazue-san, but I suspect it lies outside the High House of Light."

Chapter Eight

Mitsu had seen countless mountain villages like Fuchi Mura in his time wandering the Empire. Whether they were in Dragon lands, in the neighboring mountains of the Phoenix, on the Lion or Scorpion sides of the Spine of the World, or down in Crab territory, they consisted of a scattering of houses along a valley floor, usually near a stream that provided fresh water, the terraces of their fields rising on the slopes above.

But only a dismissive eye would assume the similarities meant they were all the same. Lion *heimin* grew rice in abundance; the Dragon and Phoenix, facing a harsher climate, grew more barley and buckwheat, and the reed-thatched roofs of their houses were steeply pitched to shed the winter snow. Crab peasants went armed to a degree that would make any other clan fear incipient rebellion.

So when Mitsu looked at Fuchi Mura, he saw the things that marked this village as distinct.

He saw a village that would not be there for long.

The declining birth rates of the Dragon meant their population had been falling steadily for generations. As their numbers shrank, the daimyō who ruled the various provinces had made the decision to draw their people inward, abandoning villages in marginal areas and consolidating the population closer to the roads and fertile valleys.

It was a pragmatic decision. But it also meant uprooting the heimin from the places where their ancestors had lived for centuries, and not all of them accepted it with grace.

Fortunately, Fuchi Mura didn't seem poised on the brink of riot. The peasants went about their work with resigned patience, while their children—fewer than they should have been—played carefree along the paths, oblivious to the worries that hung like weights over their parents' shoulders. Several of the farmhouses already stood empty, their thatching damaged by winter's storms and not repaired. The village lay fairly deep in the mountains, not convenient to anything other than the High House of Light; within a few years, Mitsu suspected, the whole place would stand empty.

In the meanwhile, it was an ideal place for Jusai, the daimyō of the Kitsuki family, to send the man she'd selected for this experiment.

The two monks had been visible on the path descending toward the village for some time before they arrived, so it was no surprise that several people waited for them just beyond the last farmhouse. One was an old woman, grey-haired but straight-backed despite her age. The other two, judging by age and one's family resemblance, were her son and her daughter-in-law.

All three bowed to the ground as Mitsu and Kazue approached. "Greetings, and welcome to Fuchi Mura, honored monks," the old woman said in a clumsy approximation of formal language. "I am Yae, the headwoman of this village. We have received word of your coming, and the honored guests whom you are to meet are waiting here for you. Please allow me to offer you the use of my humble house for as long as you wish to stay. There is plenty of room, as my husband passed into Meido this past winter."

"Please, grandmother, rise," Mitsu said. "The others as well." Once they were on their feet, he said, "I am Togashi Mitsu, and this is Togashi Kazue. We will gratefully accept your hospitality, but hope not to burden you for long."

The formalities took some time, because Mitsu didn't want to insult Yae by hurrying through them. Once he and Kazue entered the village, though, he sent the younger monk to bathe, while he sought out the people who had come to meet them.

It was a small group, just two ashigaru and a bushi, plus the man they'd brought. The bushi introduced himself with brief courtesy as Mirumoto Ujinao. "We have him in the storage shed out back," Ujinao said.

Such sheds were common in Dragon lands, where timber was abundant and the risk of burning down the main residence very real. They weren't generally used for sleeping, though, and Mitsu frowned. "'Have' him?"

"Were you not told whom we were bringing?"

Hassuno had written to Kitsuki Jusai to request someone suitable for Kazue to work on. Mitsu hadn't given a lot of thought to who that might be…but he should have.

"His name is Heidoku," Ujinao said. "And he killed a samurai."

The shed might have belonged to the village headwoman, but it hadn't been repaired in quite some time, and it wasn't locked. Out there in the hinterlands, who would break in and steal anything? Whatever items of true value Yae owned, she undoubtedly kept close. The shed was for household tools and other things she didn't want to risk losing in a fire, not for coins or finery.

The bar holding its doors shut was a recent addition, placed to not to keep thieves from breaking in, but to keep the shed's contents from escaping.

When Mitsu heaved the creaking doors open, he found the interior all but empty. The household tools had been cleared out; the only thing it held now was a man, curled up against the back wall with his bound hands before him.

Even if Ujinao hadn't told him the story, Mitsu would have known this man was a peasant. Samurai, better fed and cared for by skilled physicians, tended to grow taller and straighter than the heimin, and kept more of their teeth. The scars Heidoku bore weren't those of a bushi who had seen regular combat. And a samurai—even one stripped of their family name and cast out as rōnin—would have gathered themselves upright at the sight of Mitsu, holding onto what scraps of dignity remained.

Heidoku remained slumped against the wall. Only the flinch of his eyes at the sudden flood of light betrayed any reaction.

Mitsu paused, considering. Then he sat down cross-legged on the threshold, resting his hands on his knees. "Tell me your story."

Silence fell. Finally Heidoku said, "What?"

No courtesies. No attempt to bow, no polite invocation of "samurai-sama." Why should Heidoku bother? He'd committed murder; the penalty for that was death. If he hadn't been brought here, he would have been hanged by now. The man must know that this journey wasn't any kind of pardon, just a trip to some different punishment.

Whether that would prove true or not depended on Kazue's tattoo.

"Your crime," Mitsu said. "I want you to tell me about it."

The prisoner closed his eyes and turned his face away, doing his best to ignore his unwelcome intruder. Undeterred, Mitsu said, "I am told you killed a samurai. Mirumoto Oribe."

Heidoku spat. The insult was as deliberate as the lack of courtesy. Mitsu suspected he was hoping to outrage someone enough to provoke a swifter death. What had they told him about the reason for coming to Fuchi Mura?

"Yes, I killed him," Heidoku said. "I beat his head in with the handle of my millstone. Beat it to a broken, bloody pulp, and then kept on hitting long after he was dead."

"Why?"

If Heidoku had been walking, he would have stumbled over his own feet. The law didn't care *why* a peasant killed a samurai; the cause had no effect on the sentence. For a member of the lower classes to murder a superior was an unforgivable crime. So why should someone like Mitsu bother asking?

Mitsu waited.

Bare feet scuffed against the hard-packed dirt of the floor, as if Heidoku were trying to press himself into the wall. When he spoke, his voice was softer, thinner. "He...he was beating a lad. Overseer of our village, and he made all the young ones work for him as servants, but he beat them for every little thing. Took a cane to them if his tea wasn't hot enough, if his rice was too sticky, if he found a bug crawling across his futon. Taku, the lad, he—he asked to be let off duty so he could tend to his grandmother. The bastard started cursing and laying into him, and I...I stopped him."

This wasn't the bravado of a moment before, emphasizing the grotesquerie of the murder in the hope of getting a reaction. It was the truth, told with the hopeless air of a man who was certain no one would care.

Mitsu asked quietly, "Had you reported Mirumoto Oribe's abuses?"

He suspected the answer even before a bitter laugh answered him. "The word of a miller against his samurai overseer. Who would listen to me?"

No one. In the eyes of the law, a peasant could testify against a peasant, and a samurai against a samurai, but if two people of unequal status disagreed, credence went to the higher-ranking one. In theory this was because with rank went the burden of honor, of speaking honestly even when it was to one's own detriment.

In practice, Mitsu knew, it rarely worked out that cleanly.

Murder was not the answer, of course. The harmony of the world depended on each person fulfilling their role; it could not allow for men like Heidoku deciding to take justice into their own hands. But the first failure had been Oribe's, forgetting that Bushidō exhorted him to compassion, justice, and self-control. And the second had been that of Oribe's lord, whose responsibility it was to correct his subordinates when they strayed.

The weight of those first two failures had fallen on Heidoku and everyone in his village. Under that pressure, it was unsurprising that a soul might break.

Mitsu closed his eyes. He had no fear that Heidoku would attack him, and he needed to detach himself from the sight of the man. Oribe was beyond human justice now; he would face Emma-Ō, the Fortune of Death, and reap the consequences in his next lifetime. Oribe's lord might yet be disciplined and made to reform. But Heidoku must answer for his own crime.

Compassion burned in Mitsu's heart. That must be balanced against the other virtues, though, and in this case, justice must win out.

He opened his eyes.

"You will soon face one of my sisters," Mitsu said. "Go to her with dignity. What will happen to you then, I do not know—it is in the hands of the Fortunes. You may die, as you would have done had you never been brought here. But it may be that the Heavens will choose to spare you. I recommend you spend tonight in prayer."

The flickers of life that had shown in Heidoku guttered out, and he slumped once more against the wall. This was a man who had given up on the Fortunes—or at least on their mercy for him.

Mitsu rose and left, barring the door once more. Then he walked a small distance away, struggling with himself.

Should I tell Kazue-san, or not?

He took a deep breath of the mountain air and exhaled it slowly. No. He didn't know what her tattoo would do, but now, of all times, he must not prejudice her thinking by telling her the specifics of Heidoku's crime. She knew he was a prisoner, condemned to death and then sent here, but beyond that, she must face him with nothing but instinct to guide her.

That would have to be enough.

Chapter Nine

Kazue declined breakfast the next morning, saying she had decided to fast. But the truth beneath the polite fiction was that her fast had its roots in a more mundane cause: she was too queasy with nerves to eat.

She had spent the night in the small structure that served the village as both shrine and temple. Here the people of Fuchi Mura came to make offerings to the Fortunes and hear what few parts of the Tao seemed to have relevance to their difficult lives. In this they were aided by a middle-aged monk who nominally served the Order of Ten Thousand Fortunes, but who espoused both Fortunist and Shinseist theologies without much differentiation between them. Kazue spoke briefly with him and found him unlettered yet good-hearted. Being asked to bless an ise zumi from the High House of Light reduced him to stammering, but he pulled himself together and did as she asked.

When dawn came and brought Mitsu with it, she hoped those blessings would be enough.

Her thoughts must have been not as well-hidden as she hoped, because Mitsu spoke gently. "If he had not been brought here, they would have hanged him. Even if he dies as a result of your actions today, you will have done no worse than the justice already passed down."

It wasn't much comfort. But Kazue knew her duty—and she would rather face an unpleasant answer than continue to live with uncertainty.

"Where would you like to test this?" Mitsu asked.

She almost wanted to name the little temple-shrine. If her tattoo proved lethal, though, she didn't want to defile the structure with death. And if it proved destructive…better to be somewhere well clear of the village.

"Up on the ridge," she said, shading her eyes with one hand. "Under that pine tree at the top." Her tattoo had first brought her to Kanta under a pine tree; she hoped the association would prove auspicious.

She climbed the slope ahead of the others, leaving Mitsu to notify Mirumoto Ujinao. Out in the sunlight, the wind was a welcome touch of coolness; under the pine's shading boughs, it bit more sharply. Kazue sat cross-legged in the dirt and waited, doing her best to clear her mind, and only partially succeeding.

No one spoke on the way up to her, but she heard them approaching: the muted rattle of Ujinao's armor, the soft thud of feet against the earth.

When they arrived at the top of the ridge, Kazue said, "Seat him in front of me."

The two ashigaru pushed Heidoku down. He knelt with his hands bound in front of him and his head bowed. It meant she couldn't see his expression—couldn't see his face properly at all, just a foreshortened sliver of forehead and nose—and she was shamefully glad of that. If he had looked her in the eye, she might have lost her nerve.

She could not allow such thoughts to disturb her. Kazue settled her breathing, focusing only on the rise and fall of her chest…and the power within her tattoo.

If Mitsu had asked, she would have told him the process might require hours of meditation, as it had before. This time, though, it came much more rapidly.

At first it was the familiar ripple. The sense that there was *something* in front of her—a presence, a disturbance. She could tell it came from Heidoku, and that was a relief: her tattoo's failure to work on Mitsu back at the monastery could have meant this entire experiment was in vain, Heidoku an unsuitable target. Maybe the problem before had simply been that Mitsu's distress was too deliberate, too distant, not immediate enough.

Or perhaps it was the three sins she sensed, not simply general turmoil. Kanta, hiding away under the pine tree, must have been feeling regret for the turn his life had taken. Heidoku, facing death, must be deeply within the grip of fear; peasants were not taught to face their own end with the same equanimity as a samurai.

But the three sins were fundamental because all human suffering ultimately arose from one of those sources. Mitsu might have wept out of compassion for the things he'd seen, but that was, in its own way, a form of regret.

She couldn't learn the truth by halting here. She had to draw more deeply on the tattoo's power, and see what it did when directed against a specific person.

Kazue inhaled again, a sharp, deep breath. Then she let it out, a fierce hiss like she used when training in jūjutsu, and stopped holding back.

Fear. Regret. Desire. Yes, all three of those were there; they were in every person to one degree or another, and all three were strong in Heidoku right now. His head came up, like a puppet's on a string, and she saw his blunt, scarred face, two teeth missing on one side where they had been pulled or knocked out. He desired to see the samurai suffer as his own people did: not all of them, but the ones who reaped the benefits of their rank without caring for its burdens. He regretted not protecting someone, more than one someone, not protecting them sooner or better. He feared his death, but he feared even more what unknown thing Kazue was going to do to him.

She sank deeper.

Helplessness. That was fear and regret and desire all together: the wish to act, the awareness of how impossible it was, the terror of what would happen as a consequence. And lacing through it came white-hot strands of violence, the impulse to *hurt*, the horror at what he'd done, the bone-deep terror when he'd realized.

But what *had* he done?

Did her ability go beyond sensing his inner state, the *honne* behind the tatemae? Was the effect of her tattoo to read other people's minds—to strip away that last defense of privacy?

No.

She'd described it to Mitsu as a cliff, to herself as a canyon: the feeling that there was something more, an edge she could push her target over. Now that she stood poised at its brink, she felt it as an abyss. Not a vast gulf like the valley between two mountains, but just a crack, tiny and yet infinitely deep. A flaw, an opening, and not one she would push Heidoku into; rather, it was a gap into which something else might come.

There were mediums in the rural parts of Rokugan who claimed to become possessed by kami and speak with their voices. When Kazue spoke, she might almost have mistaken her speech for that—almost. She knew the words were her own. But they spilled from her tongue like water from a hidden spring, unforeseen until the moment of their speaking.

"The wheel without a hub, turning, stops for the hand of neither master nor no master."

She spoke in a mild tone, hardly louder than a whisper, but in her mind it struck like a thunderclap. And as soon as the last word passed her lips, Kazue sagged with sudden exhaustion. She felt as if she had lifted the High House of Light on her own back and carried it to a new peak. Mitsu moved a half step forward, but stopped himself; Kazue caught her weight on one hand and refocused her eyes on Heidoku.

He blinked, brow furrowing into two vertical lines. Then he shook his head, like a dog trying to shake away a fly.

Mirumoto Ujinao said, "What happened?"

Kazue tested her voice, unsure if it would work. "I am—not sure."

"Did you do anything?" Ujinao asked, unaware of or unconcerned with his rudeness. He prodded Heidoku with one foot. "Speak! Tell us what has happened to you!"

Heidoku didn't respond. Kazue wasn't sure he'd even heard Ujinao.

She was grateful when Mitsu intervened. Kazue wasn't sure she could have stood right then if she tried, and she didn't look very commanding propped up on one hand. "Let me examine him," Mitsu said, and suited deeds to words.

But he found nothing: only that Heidoku would not, or perhaps could not, speak. "If he has only been struck mute," Ujinao said, "then that is not enough for his crime. I will take him down to the village and execute him."

"Wait," Mitsu said. "We do not know yet what the true effect of this was. Take him back, but keep him under constant watch. I will be with you as soon as I have seen to Kazue-san."

Ujinao clearly thought Mitsu was putting off the inevitable, but he nodded and snapped a command to his ashigaru. When they were safely out of earshot, Mitsu knelt at Kazue's side and said, "Are you all right?"

She nodded, unsure whether it was true or not.

"What can you tell me?"

As if that one cryptic line had stolen all her eloquence, the explanation came haltingly. She finished her account by saying, "Those words—I do not know what they were."

Mitsu eased himself into a more comfortable position. "They sounded like a kōan. Or at least the ending of one."

The ise zumi used kōan as a teaching tool, a way to help novices break through into greater understanding. But what Kazue had said was nowhere in the collections of stories and dialogues she'd studied during her training. "I am not sure. It felt almost like..." One hand started to rise toward her scalp. She made herself stop. "Like a weapon," she whispered.

"Driven into the crack you sensed." Mitsu frowned, then shook his head and rose, dusting his hands and knees clean of dirt. "Well, I suspect the answer to this question is waiting for us down in Fuchi Mura. If you can stand, we should go see."

Chapter Ten

Heidoku remained silent for the rest of the day, neither speaking to anyone, nor showing any sign that he heard them. If hauled to his feet he would walk, but he would halt as soon as his captors stopped pushing him along. When Mitsu insisted on providing the man with food, saying, "he hasn't been executed yet," Heidoku paid it no attention.

Kazue watched for a time, until she couldn't bear it any longer. Then she went back to the temple-shrine and prayed for wisdom. She had successfully used her tattoo; she still didn't know what it did.

She'd done *something*, though, and it struck a nameless fear deep within her heart. As if whatever had happened to Heidoku was…something she had seen before? Not from a similar tattoo; surely she would have found a record for it if the knot had ever appeared in ise zumi history. Something she remembered from a past life—only no matter how she reached for it, the memory slipped through her fingers like mist.

No. That made it sound inevitable, like it wasn't her fault. In truth her mind shied away from the memory, no matter how hard she tried to steel herself. Like a hand flinching away from a flame.

Because she knew that touching it would hurt.

But she made a point of thanking the Fortunes for putting Mitsu at her side. He showed no impatience or disappointment, and seemed content to observe until there was nothing more to be learned from Heidoku. By herself, Kazue didn't think she could have mustered the conviction to prevent Ujinao from hanging the prisoner, so that he could declare his duty complete and return home. Mitsu insisted they wait three days before they declared the experiment finished.

She had three days to figure out what she had done.

On the second day Heidoku began to speak.

"The wheel without a hub, turning, stops for the hand of neither master nor no master."

He mumbled it to himself, dazed at first, then thoughtfully, then with an increasingly frantic air. The words shifted, grew, as if he were attacking them from different angles: "The hubless wheel, the wheel that has no hub. It turns around nothingness, no hub, no center, empty, an empty wheel."

Mitsu and Kazue watched him, while she tried to pretend the sight wasn't making her gut twist. "How long will he go on doing this?" she whispered.

Heidoku couldn't possibly have heard her, but his head came up anyway, his gaze fixing—not on the two of them, she thought. *Through* them. "Master nor no master," he said. "No master or master. Masterless. The masterless wheel. What is the wheel with no hub?"

"At least Ujinao can't claim we're wasting time," Mitsu said. Which was not an answer, for her or Heidoku. "I'll persuade him to give us another few days."

But another few days were not needed. On the third day, Heidoku's mind broke.

Only the iron discipline of the High House of Light and Kazue's own sense of honor kept her from clamping her hands over her ears. The peasants of Fuchi Mura had no such compunctions; most of them hid inside their houses, while a few jostled to see the prisoner, held once more in Yae's storehouse. The door was open, Ujinao standing guard, and Heidoku's screaming laughter, laughing screams, broken shards of what had once been speech, echoed through the village.

Here and there, one could still make out a few words: "wheel," or "master." And, once, a clear sentence: "*Now* I understand."

Mitsu tried to calm the man, but half the time Heidoku didn't seem to notice he was there, and the other half he tried to claw at or cling to Mitsu's legs, while Kazue clenched her hands hard enough that her nails, short as they were, nearly drew blood. Finally she couldn't stand it any longer. Not caring that it was a display of weakness, she turned and fled.

She made it to the far end of the village before her foot caught on a stone and she fell. Mitsu caught up a few seconds later and dropped to his knees at her side. "Kazue-san—"

"You know what this is," she said, the words barely making it out of her throat. "We both know. We've seen it before."

Not often. It was rare in the Empire, but more common in the Dragon; rare among the Dragon, but more common in the Togashi. Only a scattered handful of cases—perhaps one in a generation; perhaps less—but the ise zumi remembered shreds of their previous lives. Kazue had seen this before.

And so had Mitsu.

He murmured, "Enlightened madness."

The shattering of a mind that comprehended the truth of the world before it was ready. Heidoku, the illiterate peasant who knew no more of spiritual truth than a few rote lines from the Tao: it took only a single tap to break him forever.

No wonder it hadn't worked on Mitsu. And Kanta…Kazue's stomach heaved as she thought of what she might have done to him.

Mitsu's tattoos rippled as he set his shoulders. "He may recover."

She scrabbled backward through the dirt, lurching to her feet. "Recover? You know he won't. No one has ever come back from enlightened madness. I told you that what I felt in him was a crack, a flaw, and I drove something into it. Like driving a wedge into a block of wood so it splits. I broke him open and I *can't undo that.*"

She was losing her composure, her voice getting higher, her speech more rapid, but she couldn't hold it in any longer. She knew her power now, and it was the power to destroy minds.

For the first time, she saw Mitsu at a loss for words. It seemed almost by reflex that he said, "Our tattoos are a gift from the Heavens. They would not have given you such a talent for no reason."

"A *talent*?" Kazue jerked back, as if tearing free of a hold he hadn't tried to take. "This isn't a thing to celebrate, senpai! You told me that whatever I did to him, it wouldn't be worse than the sentence he already faced. But this is far worse than death!"

Mitsu flinched. "Kazue-san, remain calm—"

She was far past calm. She'd destroyed a man, shattered his spirit. Because she wanted to know what she could do.

"Whatever the Heavens intended me for," she said, her body shaking from head to toe, "I can't do it. I *won't*." Kazue spun and hurled herself up the slope, not toward the ridge where she'd broken Heidoku, but away from the shrieks of the broken man.

Mitsu knelt in the village's little shrine and tried to find tranquility.

Kazue's words had struck with more force than her storm-serpent tattoo. *You told me that whatever I did to him, it wouldn't be worse than the sentence he already faced.* He'd been a fool to make such promises—to assume that he'd seen the worst that could happen to a person. Watching Heidoku's mind splinter under the obsessive weight of Kazue's words had taught him otherwise.

If this was his test, as well as Kazue's, then he had failed.

Heidoku's voice was fainter now, worn thin by constant use. Mitsu instinctively tried to block it out, then made himself stop, letting the sound wash over him. If he hoped to find any wisdom by that route, though, he was disappointed.

Enlightened madness. If that was what had happened to Heidoku, then there was no guessing what he might do now. Men and women afflicted by that condition had done whatever their splintered minds thought best: drowned themselves, laid a thousand chopsticks end to end, devoured human flesh. Heidoku could be kept under watch, made to eat and drink, his life sustained for a time…but he would not recover.

And Mitsu was prepared to fight anyone who tried to claim this was a more fitting punishment for his crime than hanging.

The only question was whether it should be now or later.

Now, Mitsu decided. The sound was tormenting the innocent people of Fuchi Mura, who had already suffered unexpectedly from the samurai presence; he would send a message with Ujinao, urging some kind of compensation for them in return. Ending Heidoku's torment wasn't cowardice, an attempt to protect himself or Kazue from the knowledge of their actions; it was compassion and justice.

He bowed to the altar and went outside to find Ujinao.

A little while later, the noise stopped.

Kazue didn't come back before sunset. Mitsu followed her tracks until he saw her in the distance, sitting cross-legged on a flat slab of stone. She looked like she was meditating, and he knew she found solace in nature. After a moment's hesitation, he went back to the village.

She needed time, he thought.

The next morning he awoke to find her futon still folded in the corner, unused. But a message was written on the floorboard in charcoal, in the same neat, tidy hand she'd used during her time in the scriptorium.

I cannot do it.

I am sorry.

Chapter Eleven

She walked at a steady pace, without direction, without any purpose other than to get away.

Ordinarily the wild beauty of the mountains brought peace to her heart. The bare stone cliffs and crags of the peaks, the tall pines and the hawks wheeling above, the icy streams cradling little pockets of wildflowers and teeming with fish. Now she barely saw any of those things. She only knew that this far north, villages were scarce. Shinseist monks of the Brotherhood came here for hermitage, to spend years contemplating the Tao without disturbance from the outside world.

She could do the same.

Just like your mother.

Kazue's sandal caught against a rock and she stumbled, catching herself with one hand on the trunk of a hemlock. She recognized it from the bark, which formed into distinctive square shapes, each one cracked away from its neighbor. Broken. The sight made her recoil, snatching her hand back as if stung.

She could run away from human society, but not from the memory of what she had done. Even the trees would remind her.

And it *was* running away. She didn't even attempt to pretend otherwise. Maybe Mitsu was right, and the Heavens had given her that tattoo for a reason; her duty was to use it for the benefit of her order and her clan. But she couldn't face the prospect of an endless line of Heidokus, people offered up as sacrifices or object lessons or things to be disposed of in the most horrifying way imaginable. However much she trusted the wisdom of her senior monks and her clan champion, she couldn't bring herself to do that again. And if Mitsu had guessed correctly about her going out into the world this lifetime, she might be ordered to serve some other lord—one with much less restraint about when she should use the tattoo.

So in one swift move, she had renounced her duty and become rōnin.

Just like she'd been born.

I should have stayed in Phoenix lands.

Kazue started walking again, but now it was as if the ghost of her mother walked alongside her. Aika had never spoken of how she became rōnin—not directly, not to her daughter. Over the years, though, the outline of it had taken shape, from the countless little dropped hints. Aika had been born to a Shiba vassal family, though Kazue didn't know which one; she'd trained as a bushi in a minor dōjō and become a guard in some higher-ranking samurai's retinue.

Until the day she was given an order and refused to obey it. Aika had walked away from everything, rather than do as her lord commanded.

Kazue hadn't even waited for the command.

I would rather give in to fear, she thought, *than live the rest of my life with even more regret than I carry now.*

The only saving grace was that she now understood her tattoo well enough to be sure she wouldn't find herself using it out of reflex. And if she stayed away from people, she wouldn't even have any suitable targets to tempt her. Animals couldn't find Enlightenment, and so they couldn't be broken by it.

So long as she remained out here, everyone would be safe.

Including her.

Kazue had been in the mountains for three days when she finally began to consider the pragmatics of her situation.

Even in summertime the nights were chill, especially for someone wearing only an ise zumi's minimal clothing. As soon as the seasons changed, she would need shelter, unless she meant to die of the cold. And Kazue knew enough of wilderness survival to realize that if she wanted any hope of staying alive past autumn, she should begin preparing right away—building a shelter, stockpiling food—and that still might not be enough. Even Shinseist hermits started their isolation with more in the way of supplies than she had.

She might have no choice but to visit at least one village, and hope she could work in exchange for a few necessary items. Like warmer clothing.

But she couldn't face the prospect, not yet. Kazue kept moving, studying the landscape around her, trying to find a spot that boasted enough wild food sources to sustain her for a good long while.

Aika had taught her some of that, long before she ever became an ise zumi. They lived in a town, and Aika earned enough to get by, but life as a rōnin was hard. She'd had to survive in the wild before, and wanted to make sure her daughter could do the same, in case it became necessary someday. When Kazue—Yanai, as she had been then—declared that she was going to the High House of Light, her mother must have thought such risks were behind her forever. *My daughter will be a clan samurai*, she had said, and buried her tears in Yanai's shoulder as they embraced.

Mother. I'm sorry. More regret for Kazue to bear, and she was only glad that the reclusive habits of the Dragon meant Aika would never know how her daughter had failed.

Samurai elsewhere in Rokugan would say that an honorable suicide was the only way for Kazue to redeem herself now. But she was an ise zumi: killing herself would only send her back to the order, a few years down the road when she was old enough to feel the call to the High House of Light. And then after they trained her again, she would undergo her gempuku, and perhaps remember the unspeakable shame of her previous life. Death was no escape from that.

On the fifth day, as Kazue was washing herself on the bank of a mountain stream, she scrubbed one hand over her scalp...then paused.

She hadn't shaved since the morning she destroyed Heidoku. Her hair was already beginning to obscure the tattoo. Soon it would cover the lines enough to prevent her from calling on its power. At that point she wouldn't have to fear using it, no matter the provocation.

At that point, no one would even know it was there.

But the storm-serpent on her right arm still proclaimed her an ise zumi. If she wore something to cover it, though—in a year or two, when her hair was long enough that nobody would realize it had once been shaved off—

She could rejoin society, and be safe.

Was that what she wanted?

Kazue sat back on her haunches, shivering slightly as a breeze dried the icy water on her skin. Although she'd tried not to think about him since the day she fled, it was as if Mitsu sat at her side, picking up the thread of the conversation they'd had on their way to Fuchi Mura. About Kazue going out into the world, and about the practice of giving ise zumi tattoos that might never see use in this lifetime.

Ise zumi lived and died with the power to shatter bone, walk through fire, or leap over castle walls, without ever doing those things outside of training. Who was to say her own power shouldn't be the same? Their sensei trained them to find the balance between contemplation and action. Perhaps she'd simply tried to call on the knot of lines too early. Perhaps in this lifetime she was meant simply to live with it—and then in some future incarnation, she would be ready to use it.

Or perhaps that was cowardice talking, masquerading as wisdom.

"How can I tell the difference?" she whispered.

Her reflection, rippling in the stream, had no answer.

She reached for her knife and, with careful strokes, scraped the stubble away. It wasn't a decision: more like a decision not to decide yet. Not to fully surrender her identity as an ise zumi, as a Togashi, as a Dragon.

She could always let it grow again.

Chapter Twelve

Mitsu waited another three days in Fuchi Mura after Ujinao left, hoping Kazue would come back.

He told the bushi that she was in seclusion after the execution of Heidoku—which was true, if not precisely honest. Mitsu was a reasonably honorable man, but if Kazue managed to pull herself together and come back, he didn't want her humiliated by a more accurate description of her absence.

He knew in his heart, though, that she wouldn't come back. Not to Fuchi Mura, anyway. He stayed three days just in case, praying in the little shrine and helping the villagers however he could. Then his own duties sent him back to the High House of Light, hoping every step of the way that he would arrive to find Kazue already there.

She wasn't.

Hassuno-sama paled visibly when he told her what effect Kazue's tattoo had on the condemned peasant. "Enlightened madness? Are you certain?"

"Yes," Mitsu said. "I remember when Togashi Shidai broke, two hundred years ago. In his case it came about from reading too deeply in the restricted scrolls, but the effect was the same."

He'd never seen the iemoto at a loss for words. She sat for some time, her expression serene once more, but it was the kind of serenity that masked turmoil within. Then she said, "And Kazue-san?"

"She needs time to think, iemoto-sama," Mitsu said. "And I think it is better that she takes that time away from the monastery and its distractions."

Hassuno-sama's gaze sharpened. "Did you instruct her to do so?"

He couldn't bring himself to lie outright to the head of his order. Kazue hadn't been seeking contemplation; she had run away, overwhelmed by her fears. And those fears weren't the kind of thing one could resolve in a few days—maybe not even in a few months.

It was entirely possible they'd lost her, at least for this lifetime.

But maybe not. She was no newcomer to the order, enduring the weight of their teachings for the first or even third time; she might find her way out from under this one. And Mitsu was still not willing to be the one who shamed her.

So he merely said, "She needs time to think."

Hassuno-sama could read through that well enough. She knew both what he was not saying and why. Instead of pressing, she asked, "And you, Mitsu-san?"

This visit to the monastery was already longer than most. But Mitsu found himself with no urge to wander off again, seeking adventure and new things in the rest of the Empire. No, what he really wanted to do was to scour the neighboring mountains until he found Kazue, and then help her.

But until he had something more useful to say to her than what he'd already said, his presence would only rub salt in an open wound.

Mitsu bowed low. "If you have need of me elsewhere, iemoto-sama, command me. Otherwise I will remain here."

"Stay," she said. "For now."

Silently, Mitsu sent a prayer of thanks up to the Fortunes. Because he could think of one person who might be able to help, and that person never left the High House of Light.

He found Gaijutsu-sensei in a tiny courtyard supervising three of his apprentices, who were hard at work grinding the pigments used to make tattoo ink. They had what looked like corroded bronze in their mortars, and the grinding seemed to be going very slowly.

A senior apprentice was kneeling nearby, ready to fetch anything his master needed. When he saw Mitsu at the gate, the apprentice rose to whisper in Gaijutsu-sensei's ear. A flick of the latter's fingers indicated that Mitsu should approach, so he bowed and obeyed.

"Sensei," he said, "I apologize for troubling you. May I speak with you privately?"

To his senior apprentice, Gaijutsu-sensei said, "Make sure they grind it finely enough." Then he stretched out his arm for Mitsu to support it and said, "Walk with me."

They moved at a slow pace out of the courtyard, into one of the gardens reserved for senior monks. Mitsu waited until they had passed into a stand of bamboo before he spoke. Elsewhere in Rokugan, he might have worried about someone eavesdropping from cover, but not in the High House of Light.

His report this time was briefer than the one he'd given to Hassuno-sama. When he was done, Mitsu asked the question that had been seething in his mind since Heidoku's mind had broken. "Sensei—is it possible that some…outside influence has corrupted Kazue's tattoo?"

Gaijutsu halted on the path, turning his blind face toward Mitsu's in astonishment. "Corrupted it?"

"Warped its power somehow. Turned what ought to have been a beneficial effect into one of pure destruction." The tattoo master had to be able to feel the tension in Mitsu's arm, knotting his muscles tight. "I know you saw that image in a vision. But I cannot understand why Tengoku would afflict her with this—what honorable purpose it could possibly serve in the world."

"Ah." Gaijutsu-sensei stood like a stone, while a gust of wind made the bamboo sway around them. By the time it died down, he seemed to have made a decision. "Come with me, Mitsu-san. There is something I think you are ready to see."

Mitsu had known for many lifetimes that the pigments and other supplies Gaijutsu-sensei used were kept in a small, freestanding building in an out-of-the-way part of the monastery.

He had never realized there was a trapdoor in the floor, opening onto a steep staircase and a dark tunnel.

Gaijutsu-sensei paused at the top of the stairs. "Oh, yes. I imagine you will want to bring a light."

Mitsu fetched a lamp and followed the tattoo master silently. He didn't need to be told that whatever he was about to see wasn't common knowledge, even among the senior ise zumi. Or that it should be kept secret afterward.

The tunnel seemed to stretch on forever, though distances became deceptive underground, with only a bobbing lamp for illumination. The stone around them was chill, and the passage narrow enough that Mitsu's shoulders kept brushing the walls. Then they came to a single door, held shut by a lock with no keyhole.

He didn't see what Gaijutsu-sensei did to open the lock. The man's body obscured it for a moment; then it clicked, and the door swung open.

The room beyond was small, and austere even by the standards of the monastery. The carvings that adorned the walls were in a style Mitsu recognized as ancient, and the cabinet that stood in the middle of the room wasn't much more recent. It was the sole object in the room.

"Ordinarily I come down here only when I am preparing to tattoo someone," Gaijutsu-sensei said. "But also, very rarely, to show someone this."

He bowed and clapped his hands as if approaching a shrine, then opened the lacquered doors of the cabinet. Inside stood a single vessel, carved from a pale stone so thin that Mitsu could see the dark liquid it contained. The stopper proved to be a long shaft, of the sort a physician or a perfumer might use to add just a drop or two to some other mixture.

In the light of Mitsu's lamp, the liquid at the end of the stopper was as red as blood.

"From Togashi-no-Kami," Gaijutsu-sensei said. "We use it in every ise zumi tattoo—every one that contains power. It is from this that the power comes."

Mitsu didn't need the explanation. The moment he saw the blood, his own skin sang in response, everywhere he had a tattoo.

The resonance crawled along his arms and legs, across his chest and back, up his neck to the dragon head that spanned his scalp.

His ability to withstand blows, to transform his hands into claws, to run faster than the wind and breathe fire at his enemies… they all derived from the Kami who had founded his clan, his family, and his order.

No force short of Fu Leng himself could corrupt that.

The thought made Mitsu's skin shudder in a different way. He'd traveled from one end of the Empire to the other, and while he'd spent a good deal of that time among the common people, he'd also encountered certain kinds of Crab and Phoenix samurai: those who hunted the practitioners of a particular blasphemous art.

His mouth refused to shape the words *blood magic*. But Gaijutsu-sensei was alert to things other than sight; he must have heard Mitsu's breath catch. The tattoo master restoppered the vial. "We keep this secret for many reasons," he said. "There are those who would seek to exploit it, to capture this power for themselves…and there are those who would misunderstand."

Mitsu couldn't stop the puff of incredulous laughter that escaped him. Explaining to a Kuni Witch Hunter or an Asako Inquisitor that *this* blood magic didn't call on the power of Jigoku…yes, they would misunderstand. Quite a lot.

Whereas Mitsu himself was beginning to understand even more. "Your visions," he said. "They come from Togashi-no-Kami, don't they? So whatever is happening with Kazue…is meant to be."

Gaijutsu-sensei inclined his head, then placed the vial back in the cabinet and closed the doors, bowing to them once more. This time Mitsu followed his lead.

His muscles ached, fighting themselves. He wanted more than anything to charge back down the tunnel and out of the monastery, into the wilderness where Kazue had vanished. The tattoo she bore—it wasn't just dangerous to other people. Enlightened madness appeared more often among the ise zumi because of their order's practices, because the power they carried in their skin was sometimes too much for them to bear. If she didn't find a balance with the lines inked into her scalp, they might wind up breaking her the same way they'd broken Heidoku.

But now Mitsu had information that could help her. If she knew the tattoo she bore truly was a gift, a sign of great honor from the Kami himself—

Would that help? Or would it make the danger worse?

He didn't know. And in some ways it didn't matter, because what Gaijutsu-sensei had shown him here was secret. Mitsu had no right to share that with anyone else. And as desperately as he wanted to help Kazue...

In the end, she would have to find her way out of the wilderness on her own. It wasn't enough for her to trust Togashi-no-Kami's wisdom; she had to trust *herself*. Without that, she would always be vulnerable.

Someone with that kind of power could not afford to be vulnerable.

A blind man's eyes did not fix themselves on any particular target, but Mitsu knew Gaijutsu-sensei was watching him. Waiting, just as Hassuno-sama had, to see what he would do.

Was the right answer to stay, or to go?

Ordinarily he would have gone in a heartbeat. But although his actions until now had brought him to the attention of the monastery's leaders, Mitsu suspected they were looking for more.

It doesn't matter what they're looking for. You need to do what is right for this situation.

As much as it galled him to admit it, what was right in this case was inaction.

The decision washed down his limbs like cool water. In every lifetime, this had been the hardest lesson for Mitsu to learn: not what to do, but what *not* to do. How to recognize when it was better to remain still, rather than to act. How to accept that inaction could be the right course.

They hadn't assigned him to Kazue to help solve her problems. They'd done it to teach him that those problems were hers to solve—not his.

Mitsu followed Gaijutsu-sensei back down the corridor and into the light. Then he extinguished the lamp, thanked the tattoo master, and went to pray.

Chapter Thirteen

Kazue kept shaving her head after that. It became her way of marking time, in a place where time seemed almost to become an illusion: the weather changed, sun to clouds and back again, and flowers bloomed and died, but it was easy to pretend the mountain summer would go on forever. The scrape of her knife over her scalp reminded her that the real illusion was that feeling of timelessness. Sooner or later, she would have to take steps to ensure her ongoing survival—or else return to the monastery.

But as the days went on, that second possibility faded further and further from her mind.

Her voice had destroyed Heidoku. The power came from the tattoo, but if that were the guiding hand, her voice was the weapon. The last words she'd spoken were in Fuchi Mura, before she fled; since then she had been silent. Even the mental conversations she had with herself were fading away, replaced by a state of mind that was neither meditation nor normal activity. She moved without thinking, following instinct as she searched for water, food, shelter. Like a bird, or the wolves that came down from the peaks when winters grew hard, preying on livestock and even people.

She wasn't going to become a predator, but that way of thought was comfortable. Birds didn't have to remember the past. Wolves didn't feel guilt for what they'd done.

Her movements loosened, abandoning the smooth control of a well-trained monk in favor of something more feral. When she heard the grunting of a bear, she sank reflexively into a crouch, then skittered like an insect from cover to cover until she was downwind of the creature and could flee. At night she curled tight for warmth and stayed like that until dawn, when she eased the kinks out with a few grunts of her own.

She was hungry all the time, even with her knowledge of how to find food in the wild. But it didn't bother her.

She kept washing herself in streams, though, and sharpening her knife, and shaving her head when her hair grew too long. She knew, without ever admitting it to herself, that the day she stopped doing that would be the day she surrendered her final link to the world of humanity.

Despite everything, she wasn't quite ready to do that.

Then, one morning when she had just shaved her head again, she smelled woodsmoke.

Wildfires were a danger in the summer months. If the season was too dry, a lightning strike could set the trees aflame, and then the winds would carry the sparks and the blaze faster than anyone could run without the aid of a tattoo.

Those thoughts made her think of Mitsu, for the first time in days—Mitsu whose centipede tattoo carried him faster than thought, Mitsu who had breathed fire against fire to deprive it of fuel and save the monastery from danger.

She lacked fire and speed both. But after one blank moment of animal alertness, human sense reasserted itself: the scent was a mere thread, the product of a small fire, not a blaze that would consume the mountains. And there had been no lightning strikes.

Someone was out here.

In my mountains.

That thought—the first articulate one she'd had in some time—recalled Kazue to herself. It was absurd to think of the mountains as her own; she wasn't some territorial beast, and neither was she a bandit, trying to assert some kind of claim against samurai and the Emperor. She was…

I'm human. That's enough for now.

But she remained wary as she approached the source of the smoke. It was coming from the direction of a bald-topped peak, but lower on its slope. Kazue took care to remain downwind and behind brush that would hide her from prying eyes. Finally she crept close enough to catch a glimpse of the smoke itself and the fire it came from, burning in a shallow earthen pit in front of a hut.

Kazue crouched beneath the low-hanging branch of a tree, balancing herself with fingertips braced in the dirt as she peered around. She saw no movement, apart from the dance of the flames. No sensible person would leave a fire unattended for long, though, even if they had dug out the pit so nothing nearby would catch. That was the *other* way wildfires got started.

Then again, foolish hermits were always a possibility. Just because someone decided to contemplate the Tao on the edge of the Empire didn't mean they knew the first thing about surviving in the wilderness.

The darkness inside the hut shifted, and Kazue recoiled further beneath the tree. The shift resolved itself into a human figure: a woman, ducking out from under the low lintel with a simple clay pot in her hands. She went to the fire and spread the branches with another stick until she could nestle the pot in the embers. Then she sat back on her haunches and waited.

A tantalizing scent rose from the pot. Nothing elaborate, and no meat; Kazue hadn't tasted meat since she arrived at the High House of Light. But it was more than the simple roots and berries and mushrooms she'd been eating, and her mouth began to water.

To distract herself, she studied the woman. Her first assumption had been that the stranger was a religious hermit, but if so, she had forsaken the robes of her order, and hadn't cut her hair in years. She wore a homespun kimono that had been patched more than once, and leggings tied tight around her calves for practicality. Her feet were bare and her hair pulled back into a simple tail, bound at several points along its length to keep strands from escaping.

The woman wrapped her hands in her sleeves and removed the pot from the faded embers. Kazue twitched in surprise—she hadn't realized how much time had passed. Her sudden movement jarred the branch under which she sat, and the woman's head came up like a deer's, searching the trees.

Retreating would only risk giving her position away more clearly. Kazue remained where she was, scarcely breathing, until the woman relaxed. Once the stranger was fully absorbed in eating her meal, Kazue slipped away, going back to her roots and berries and mushrooms.

That should have been the end of it.

Wasn't the whole point of coming out here to avoid people? She had found a person; now the sensible thing to do would be to move onward, continuing her search for a place to settle down that would keep her fed.

Except the sight of that hut, ramshackle as it was, reminded Kazue that her current method of survival wasn't good enough. She needed shelter. She needed supplies, like a clay pot. And although she had absolutely no intention of trying to join forces with the stranger, perhaps that woman could offer her useful advice. It looked like she'd been out there a long time—longer than a single summer. She would know how to live through the winter.

It was like shaving her head. Kazue didn't make up her mind to leave, but she also didn't approach the stranger. She just kept going back to the hut, finding different hiding spots that still allowed her to see, watching the stranger go about her business.

That went on for days. *This is absurd,* Kazue told herself one morning, after she took shelter in the branches of another tree. *I have to make a decision.*

She touched her scalp. Her hair wasn't quite long enough yet to hide the tattoo, but in a few more days it would be. Once the knot was safely hidden, Kazue decided, she would speak to the stranger.

The woman was outside again, cooking in the pot, but she also had a pile of dandelion greens and other things Kazue couldn't make out at her side. She poked a finger into the pot to test its temperature and nodded in satisfaction.

Then she lifted her head and called out, "If you are hungry, you're welcome to join me. I have enough for two."

Chapter Fourteen

This time Kazue had more self-control. She didn't jerk or make any noise. After a moment, the woman added, "If not, I understand, and go in peace. But you are welcome here at any time."

It was the first human speech she'd heard in…Kazue realized she had lost count of the days. Lost count of the times she'd shaved her scalp, even. Long enough that the sound of a voice came as a shock, and she wasn't even sure her own would work in reply.

I told myself I would do this. It's coming a little early, is all.

Her body had locked tight with surprise when the woman spoke; now she made her muscles relax. One careful movement at a time, she descended from the tree, and came into the open.

Judging by the woman's reaction, she hadn't only known Kazue was present—she'd known exactly where Kazue was. She got up, dusting off her hands, and bowed. It had none of the practiced grace of a samurai's childhood training and her accent betrayed her peasant origins, but she carried herself with dignity nonetheless. "I am Senzai. Please, join me. My hospitality may be simple, but I offer you everything I have."

Kazue bowed and opened her mouth to reply—and choked. *Togashi Kazue? Or just Kazue?* Her arms were still bare; Senzai could see the storm-serpent on her right biceps, even if she missed the knot half-hidden beneath the stubble. And Kazue's clothing was clearly that of a warrior monk.

But did she have any right to claim the Togashi name, when she'd walked away from her duty?

When the pause threatened to stretch for too long, Senzai said, "I am sorry that I do not have any kind of mat or cushion, but I promise you that the grass is soft."

Kazue could feel herself flushing in embarrassment and gratitude as she knelt without giving any name at all. Senzai portioned out the food, giving Kazue what appeared to be her only bowl, and eating her own meal directly out of the pot. The soup was thin, but rich in comparison to what Kazue had been eating since Fuchi Mura, and it was all she could do not to just pour the entire thing straight down her throat.

She made herself pause halfway through to ask, "Are you a monk?"

Senzai looked startled. "No. Why do you ask?"

Kazue gestured with the bowl. "No meat. You seem to be very good at surviving out here, so I doubt it's because you don't know how to set snares."

"Ah." Senzai divided up the greens, giving Kazue the larger pile. "No, I'm simply a peasant woman. From Seseki Mura, in Kinenkan Province."

Not a village Kazue had ever heard of, but Kinenkan Province lay to the south and east of the High House of Light, and was ruled by the Agasha family. "Why did you leave?" Then she flushed again. "I am sorry. It has been…some time since I had anyone to speak with."

Senzai's gentle smile made her feel less awkward. "It's an understandable question. A peasant like me isn't generally free to leave her village and make her home in the wilderness—not unless she first takes holy orders."

The smile faded. Kazue expected to see sadness beneath: whatever drove this woman forth clearly could not have been a happy event. But Senzai seemed to have found peace with her past, because she set the pot down, folded her hands in her lap, and spoke tranquilly. "I'm told by my elders that I was always an insight-ful child, even before I could talk. My father passed away when I was only a year old, but I seemed always to know when my mother was grieving for him, and what to do to comfort her—whether that was a hand on her cheek, a silly trick to make her smile, or some misbehavior, so that she would have something to chide me for."

Kazue inhaled, holding back the tears that threatened to prick at her eyes. She knew now why she'd been watching Senzai from the shadows: because she felt kinship with this woman, another hermit seeking solace in the isolation of the mountains. But she hadn't expected this additional step, both of them fatherless chil-dren with only their mothers to raise them.

She's a peasant. I'm a rōnin. Her father died; mine abandoned my mother. The similarity wasn't as great as she thought. After days of solitude, though, every whisper of connection felt like a shout.

"You may think this is coincidence," Senzai went on, "or just the bond of a daughter to her mother. But when I learned to speak, it became more. I had a reputation in the village for always knowing when someone was secretly angry at another person, or planning a surprise. The young people came to me to ask whether the one they hoped to marry had any feelings for them in return, and whether their parents would approve. I didn't know everything—no matter what they said about me—but I knew enough."

It wasn't difficult to see how that might have gone wrong. "They came to fear you," Kazue said.

"What is charming in a child becomes more worrisome as she grows. No one likes to have their guilt revealed—their little adul-teries and thefts, a man swearing to his wife that he has stopped drinking when in truth he keeps a jug of sake behind the woodpile. And I knew that…" Senzai's gaze was distant, looking past Kazue to the trees, and beyond. "But it was difficult for me to distinguish between insight and knowledge, to realize that what seemed so plain to me was hidden from others."

Kazue's mouth was dry. "How—how did you know these things?"

Senzai met her gaze briefly, then looked down before it could become rude. "I'm not a shugenja, I promise you. And I didn't know people's thoughts. It was simple observation—simple to me, at least. The man who drank would bring in smaller loads of wood than he was capable of carrying, so that he had to go out to the woodpile more often. And he chewed more mint leaves than anyone else in the village, to hide the smell of the sake on his breath."

Not like her tattoo, then. Kazue hadn't spent enough time around Heidoku to observe anything about him, and he'd been silent and frozen when he came before her. What she knew had come from the tattoo itself, sensing the vulnerabilities that could break him. But still, it raised the hairs on the back of her neck.

Especially when Senzai went on to add, in a thoughtful tone, "Even beyond those bits of evidence…I could tell he felt guilty. I saw it in his every movement. Just as you can see that someone's angry, when they clench their fists and walk heavily and glare at the target of their anger—it was always that clear to me, even when it wasn't so obvious. I knew he felt guilty about something by looking at him; I knew what he was guilty of by looking at what he did."

Another silence descended. Kazue might not have such natural insight, but she could tell the purpose of this pause was to give her a chance to speak. Senzai couldn't possibly fail to guess that an ise zumi living in the wilderness who choked on whether to give her name might have some weight burdening her heart.

But Kazue took long enough to find her tongue that once again, Senzai filled the breach before it could grow uncomfortable. She said, "In the end, I revealed one thing too many. My neighbors began to insist I wasn't a girl at all but a yōkai, masquerading in human form. I knew they were planning to hurt me, so I fled. I lived for a time as a beggar in a nearby town, until a *yoriki* came to arrest me for vagrancy. I told him that his superior magistrate would soon find out he was in the pay of a local gang, and while he was in shock from that, I ran again. Since then, I've been out here."

"And have you never thought about going back?"

It almost felt like the cryptic phrase she'd spoken to Heidoku, with her mouth moving as if of its own accord. But in this case, Kazue knew exactly why she said it.

She hoped that in Senzai's life, she might find some guidance for her own.

Without even a breath of hesitation, Senzai shook her head. "I am done with human society," she said. "It has no need of me."

Chapter Fifteen

Senzai might be done with human society, but without ever saying it outright, she invited Kazue to stay—at least for the night.

It began with her offering to build up the fire so that Kazue could wash properly, with gritty sand to scrub herself down. For the first time since Fuchi Mura, Kazue felt like she was truly clean, and without thinking she found herself shaving her head again. By now her scalp was red and irritated from shaving so often in cold water, though she'd tried to keep her knife in good condition; it would have been better to let her skin heal for a while. But it was habit now, until she made up her mind once and for all. And despite what Senzai had said, she hadn't done that quite yet.

She was one step closer to it, though. A life like Senzai's seemed appealing: no challenges except survival, no obligations except to herself. She might be fated to return to the ise zumi in her next lifetime, but in this one, she could find peace through solitude.

Heating the water used up a lot of the firewood. "I'll gather more later," Senzai said, but Kazue insisted on helping, in gratitude for her hospitality. Together they went out into the forest, collecting armfuls of branches and carrying them back to the hut.

"I apologize for lurking around like that," Kazue said as they walked.

"There's nothing to apologize for. I'm a stranger out in the woods; naturally you would be wary."

Kazue ran her thumb over the scab forming where she'd scraped her left forearm across a stone. "Wary, yes—but it was more than that. I…I have always enjoyed being out in the natural world. Left to myself, I think I enjoy it a little too much."

"What do you mean, too much?" Senzai braced her foot against a fallen branch and pulled, snapping it into two pieces of more convenient size.

The branch had a cousin, equally dead, but still attached to the tree. Kazue jumped and wrapped her hands around it, then hung there, bouncing slightly. "Even though I have not been out here as long as you, it has changed how I think."

"Is that a bad thing?"

Her weight finally tore the branch loose, and Kazue thumped to the ground in a shower of dead leaves. "It was like…nothing existed but the present moment. I was trying not to think about the past or the future, and the result was that they faded from my mind. I started to act more like an animal, on instinct."

Senzai bent to help her break the branch into pieces. "Yes, I know what you mean." She grunted as the wood gave way. "When there's no one to talk to, there's no need to put your thoughts into words. Without words, past and future lose their separate nature. You act based on your knowledge and according to your need, without conscious thought. But again—is that a bad thing?"

Kazue stopped in the midst of brushing bark from her hands. *Without conscious thought*: it was one of the lessons of jūjutsu, of any martial training. To fight with the conscious mind was too slow: perception, analysis, and decision paralyzed the body and gave the opponent time to strike. The movements of a true master were informed by past experience and by future intent, but the mind existed only in the present moment, and acted without conscious thought.

"I suppose not," she said slowly, collecting the pieces. "I had not considered it that way."

"The natural state of the mind is to be at peace," Senzai said, continuing onward. "It's only when we allow external things to trouble us that we lose that serenity."

That wasn't the only such thing she said during the course of the day. The branches they'd gathered were useful, but they would burn fairly quickly, and Senzai didn't have an ax to cut heavier logs. When they came upon an entire young beech tree that had fallen on a slope, Kazue offered to do what she could to break it up. After stripping the smaller limbs with ordinary strikes, she set her feet and breathed, focusing her attention, for the first time in weeks, on the storm clouds and winding serpent inked into her right arm.

Her first attempt produced a spray of bark and rolled the trunk halfway down the slope, but didn't break the wood. While Senzai watched, Kazue descended and this time placed herself beneath the trunk, so that at least she would knock it upward, rather than down into an inaccessible gulch.

Laughter brightened Senzai's voice as she called out, "Don't try so hard! Strike without effort, like you did at the branches."

Kazue paused, shading her eyes with one hand as she looked up to where Senzai perched on a comfortably rounded boulder. "Are you sure you were not a monk at some point?"

"Quite sure! You would know better than me, but I assume becoming a monk is the sort of thing a person would remember."

"Maybe you were one in a previous life, then," Kazue said, lining herself up with the tree. "Or you are just living proof of what Shinsei said—that the Eternal Truth can be found anywhere, even in a single drop of water. You have never studied the Tao, but you understand its principles better than some monks I have known."

Strike without effort. She hadn't practiced enough with the storm cloud tattoo, her attention at first focused too much on the knot and its mysteries, then trying to avoid all thought of her tattoos entirely. But she already knew her use of the storm-serpent could be refined, and the only danger it posed right now was to the tree.

No, Kazue thought. *No danger.* And she struck.

She'd thought once that her tattoo might let her shatter a tree. She knew now that she could—but that wasn't what happened. Instead she cleaved off a piece of the trunk about the length of her forearm, not as cleanly as an ax would have, but well enough to leave a usable log. A few strikes later, the whole trunk had been sectioned into useful pieces, good solid hardwood that could sustain Senzai's fire for many hours.

Senzai came down to join her and bowed in gratitude. "I'll come and collect these tomorrow."

"No need," Kazue said. "Let us take the smaller branches with us, and then I will come back for these. And then—" She glanced down at herself and laughed. "I think I will need to bathe again."

She contented herself with rinsing off in a stream, rather than burning more wood for another hot bath. Once all the large logs were stacked up under a sheltering tree where they wouldn't get too wet if it rained, Senzai set about preparing the evening meal, with Kazue's assistance.

They didn't talk the whole time. Senzai was even more content than Kazue to work in silence, asking for things with gestures as much as words. But when Kazue drew her out briefly on this topic or that one, her impression of the hermit's wisdom deepened.

It wasn't that Senzai knew the Tao, not in the way people normally used the word. She didn't know the actual text of the Little Teacher's conversation with the Kami at the dawn of the Empire, the rules he set forth for monastic communities, and the later material written by the first abbots of the Brotherhood's orders, discussing the spiritual relationships between Shinsei's teachings, kami worship, the ancestors, the Five Elements, and the Spirit Realms. Senzai was illiterate; she couldn't have read that text even if she'd possessed a copy.

But Kazue knew full well that the book called the Tao was, as the proverb had it, not the Tao. The text was a guidebook; the Tao itself was a way. And whether it was because of her remarkable insight, or the trials she'd suffered, or her solitude in the mountains, Senzai understood that way very well.

It made Kazue wonder about her own path here. The similarities she'd noticed between Senzai's life and her own—were those mere coincidence, Kazue craving fellowship after so much time alone? Or were they signs from the Heavens, that she had come to where she needed to be?

Here, perhaps, she had found the teacher she so desperately needed.

As dusk fell, Kazue asked why Senzai kept to a vegetarian diet, despite not being a monk. The hermit said, "I know it would be easier for me to keep myself fed if I were willing to eat the flesh of animals—fish especially. But I can't bring myself to say that my own survival should come at the expense of another creature like that. I'm just one woman; why should my life matter more than that of a rabbit?"

"You are higher in the Celestial Order than a rabbit," Kazue pointed out.

"That's both true and an illusion. In a previous life, I may have *been* a rabbit. Better to live in harmony with all things, so that when I find myself in such a position, I can hope for others to live in harmony with me." Senzai prodded the fire with a long stick and added a little more fuel. "Besides, it would tempt me to see the success of my snare as an achievement, and then I would be celebrating the death of another living creature. Every victory is a funeral."

Her words struck unexpectedly home. Heidoku would have died either way, hanged for his crime regardless of what Kazue did or did not do—but her victory, uncovering the true power of her tattoo, was from another perspective a thing to mourn.

"Senzai-san." Kazue hesitated, well aware that her tongue had almost shaped it into *sensei* instead. "There are many monks in the Empire with less wisdom than you have. I know you said that the world has no need of you…but in this one thing, you are wrong. I beg you to consider returning. I know the Brotherhood would welcome you with open arms."

The hermit woman's expression remained serene, but now it was the serenity of polished stone. "No. I have left all that behind."

Without thinking, Kazue edged back from the fire until she could bow with her forehead to the ground. It didn't matter that Senzai was a peasant and Kazue a samurai; here in the wilderness, such distinctions were as meaningless as those between a human and a rabbit. "Then please accept me as your student. Tengoku has sent me here, I am sure of it. Under your tutelage, I will learn how to carry the burden I have been given."

She heard nothing, only the crackle of the fire. Then a faint rustle, as Senzai stood.

"I have left all that behind," Senzai repeated. "I ask nothing of the world beyond this place, and I owe it nothing in return. You are welcome to stay the night, but in the morning, you should go."

Chapter Sixteen

Despite her cold response, Senzai's hospitality remained undiminished. When Kazue tried to say she could leave that night, the hermit insisted she stay; when Kazue tried to cede the hut's minimal comforts to her host, Senzai insisted that she accept them. The futon was merely a blanket over dried grass, but it was softer than the ground outside, and Kazue felt guilty as she stared into the darkness, broken by threads of moonlight that came through the cracks in the walls. It might not be luxury, but of the two of them, she was the monk. The hard ground should have been *her* bed.

And it wasn't as if the comfort of the hut were helping her sleep. She lay awake, listening to the wind, and wondered: *Where did I go wrong?*

The question provoked a silent, bitter laugh. Where, indeed. There were so many points to choose from: not just here, but in Fuchi Mura, at the High House of Light, all the way back through her life—not just this one, but those that had come before. Mitsu thought the knot tattoo was a gift, earned by her merit in a previous incarnation, but maybe it was a punishment for some failing.

Looking at the recent past, though…she truly had believed she was meant to find and learn from Senzai. Instead the hermit had rebuffed her, and Kazue couldn't understand why. How could someone with Senzai's compassion, her insight, cut herself off so thoroughly from the world?

The ise zumi studied the Tao, even if they didn't follow it as the Shinseist orders of the Brotherhood did. Kazue knew it advocated nonattachment—but surely there was a difference between renouncing desire and making oneself insensible to the good one could do.

Outside the ramshackle hut, the wind picked up. Kazue sighed and shifted position, arranging herself as comfortably as she could. It wasn't part of their gempuku, but one of the skills ise zumi were expected to master during their training was the ability to put themselves to sleep at will. She closed her eyes and was about to begin the meditative technique when she felt a draft and sensed a faint increase in the light against her eyelids. The blanket that covered the doorway had been pushed aside.

Senzai. Kazue drew breath to apologize…but a gutteral whisper stopped her short.

"You are unworthy."

Kazue shot upright. A figure blocked the doorway, stoop-shouldered, wild-haired, its eyes glowing with the sickly light of swamp gas. One hand held the curtain out of the way; the other scraped down the edge of the doorway, claws against weathered wood.

"You scorn your gifts, and lack the wisdom to use them well. You must be destroyed."

Hoarse and twisted though it was, Kazue recognized that voice. She breathed, *"Senzai-san."*

There were stories of this in Dragon lands, and among the Phoenix, too. Anywhere wilderness and deep religious dedication came together. Female monks, shugenja, priestesses—women dedicated to their spiritual development—went out into the mountains and the forests to cultivate their inner power. And they succeeded.

But in cutting themselves off from human society, from their duty to the world, they transformed themselves. Gradually, one silent summer and frozen winter at a time, they lost their humanity and became yōkai.

Senzai was a *kobukaiba*: a hag of the deep woods.

Kazue scrambled to her feet. "Senzai-san," she said, her hands out in a defensive gesture. "Forgive me. I should not have disturbed you—"

"*You disturb the balance of the world!*" The hut's interior fell into shadow as the kobukaiba dropped the curtain. "*I feel it in your skin, little monk. The power you don't understand, the power you fear. You have failed. You are unworthy. And I will destroy you!*"

Her voice rose to an unearthly shriek. Kazue dodged instinctively, and felt the air shift as Senzai's claws raked through the air where she'd been. She tried to twist past, gaining the doorway and the freedom of the night beyond, but wire-thin whips lashed across her face and arms—the kobukaiba's hair. It tried to wrap around her limbs, and Kazue, writhing free, slammed against the wall of the hut. The space was tiny; it gave her no room to maneuver. An instant later the hair had her trapped, ensnaring her arms so she couldn't pull loose.

The glowing eyes fixed on her, drawing nearer. "*You are full of fear, full of regret. How can a creature like you claim understanding? You are more ignorant than the most foolish child—and more dangerous.*"

"I don't want to hurt you, Senzai-san," Kazue said through clenched teeth. "But I understand this much: that the willow survives where the oak tree falls."

She stopped pulling away from the tangling hair and instead gave in, driving her fist forward—with all the power of the storm-serpent tattoo backing it.

A thunderclap broke the air. The kobukaiba shrieked as she flew backward, through the wall of the hut, into the moonlight beyond. The hair trapping Kazue went limp as it tore free from its mistress. She leaped into the new gap and saw Senzai rising at the edge of the trees, and offered up a brief prayer of thanks to the kami and the Fortunes. That blow would have shattered an ordinary woman, but yōkai were more resilient.

Because she didn't want to kill Senzai. The woman's spiritual power was very real; if it weren't, she never would have transformed into a kobukaiba. Come sunrise, she would be as patient and hospitable as before, with no memory of what she had done in the night.

But dawn was hours away. How could Kazue survive that long?

She ran up the slope, away from Senzai, wishing briefly that she had practiced the spiritual technique that would allow her to leap up the mountain in soaring bounds. If she could lose her attacker in the woods, then she might return by daylight and try to find a way to restore Senzai to humanity. Unfortunately, the scream that split the air behind her said it wouldn't be that easy.

Kazue ran harder than she ever had in her life, heedless of the danger ahead, because the danger behind was worse. The shadows around her swam into sharper detail, as if she had borrowed the vision of a cat; once she had known how to invoke such blessings, and now the memory came back to her. It let her plant her feet with more surety, keeping just ahead of the kobukaiba, for whom the darkness was her natural home.

But it wasn't enough. Kazue would tire; the yōkai would not. She used every trick she could think of, every unexpected swerve into a narrow gully and leap down a sharp but survivable drop, rolling as she hit and coming to her feet nicked in half a dozen places by the stones that had raked her. Behind her, the kobukaiba howled at the scent of blood, condemning it as impure, Kazue herself as a source of defilement.

She found herself trapped on a narrow ridge, the trees to her left too thickly placed to let her move among them with speed, the ground to her right a lethal cliff. Kazue ran up and up and up, knowing it offered no kind of escape, but bereft of other options.

And then she came to the top, and realized she had no options at all.

The ground there leveled out, but the safety it offered was an illusion. This was the bald-topped peak above Senzai's hut, and the ridge she'd taken to its summit was the only traversable path. Unless she could dredge out of her past life memories the knowledge of how to fly, she had run herself into a corner from which there was no escape.

If she had ever known how to do that, she didn't retrieve it before the kobukaiba appeared.

Up here, the mountain winds whipped Senzai's hair into a snarled net, fanning out to either side of her like wings. Her face was gaunt, cheeks sunken like those of an ascetic who had fasted for a year. Even her clothing had transformed, becoming looser and more tattered. The unhealthy light of her eyes shone brighter than the moon, and she extended her claws as if preparing to tear Kazue's soul from her body.

This is what I would become.

The realization chilled her to the bone. If Kazue somehow escaped and remained in the mountains, hiding herself away as she had considered, then eventually she would meet the same fate as Senzai. Her spiritual power would grow and turn inward, warping into the malevolence of a kobukaiba, seeking to destroy anything that threatened the balance of the world…which meant any human life that came within her reach.

But what was the alternative? To return to the ise zumi and use a power she dreaded, shattering people's spirits in blind obedience to Heaven's will? Heidoku's screams echoed in her memory, weaving through the kobukaiba's snarls like veins of blood.

Or this, right here. To stand her ground and let Senzai kill her, and hope she could solve this riddle in her next life.

I'm not ready to die. That wasn't fear talking; it was determination. Whatever Tengoku intended for her, she wanted to do it in this life. And that meant she had to survive this moment.

She *could* kill the hag. A yōkai like this was dangerous, but not against a tattooed monk—especially not one with the power of the storm in her hands. Unleashing that, though, would mean annihilating the great promise of Senzai's wisdom.

Her only other weapon was the knot.

The kobukaiba laughed, a low, skeletal sound. "*You will tear yourself apart. You cannot wield what you bear without destroying yourself—and you know it.*"

It was true. But Kazue feared destroying herself less than she feared destroying Senzai.

Unless…

Unless Tengoku intended me to use it, not against people like Heidoku, but against creatures like this.

What would enlightened madness do to a yōkai?

Kazue didn't know. But she had spent lifetime after lifetime in the High House of Light, all to learn one fundamental lesson: how to recognize the correct moment in which to unleash her power.

She set her feet against the peak of the mountain, formed her hands into an interlocking mudra, and as the kobukaiba swept toward her, invoked her tattoo.

Chapter Seventeen

The world went away.

There was no mountain, no wind, no moon, no stone. No malevolent hag seeking to destroy her.

Only understanding.

She saw without seeing. A cup was before her, plain glazed clay, all the more beautiful for its simplicity—but it was cracked.

She knew those cracks well. The same ones marred her own spirit: power, and the fear of misusing it. Senzai's insight, with her from childhood, was more than simply observation; it was the legacy of previous incarnations, past merit manifesting as ability in the present.

But people did not welcome insight, whatever they claimed. They feared it, resented it, drove it away. And so Senzai had withdrawn, not out of selfishness, but out of generosity, because she had not wished to hurt anyone.

Her caution had only made things worse. She was still human… but if she continued as she was, she would transform irredeemably into a kobukaiba, and be lost forever.

The cracks were there, in Kazue's grasp. Without hands, she held the cup, and knew she could widen its flaws. Drive them fully open, breaking the clay. Just as she had done to Heidoku.

Just as she had done to herself, once upon a time.

The interlacing knot of her tattoo wasn't a reward for past merit, the way Mitsu thought. No, Tengoku had given her the power to shatter minds because her own had once been shattered: because in a previous life she had spent so much time in meditation, seeking the truth of existence, that she'd fallen to enlightened madness. She knew its beauty and its horror alike—the purity of understanding the world, and the agony of collapsing beneath that unbearable weight.

But a broken cup could be repaired.

There was a hut for the tea ceremony at the High House of Light. Kazue had once assisted a senior monk who received a guest from the Crane Clan, and he had used an ancient set of cups mended by the technique of *kintsugi*: fusing the pieces together with a lacquer into which the artisan had blended gold dust. Kintsugi did not try to hide the damage; instead, it transformed those wounds into a new kind of beauty, golden lines threading through the surface of the clay.

Yes, she could break minds. The difference lay in the material she worked with. Heidoku had not been ready for the insight she gave, and so it destroyed him.

But Senzai was different.

Kazue spoke without a voice, without words.

"The last and the first—are they not the same?"

This was the truth:

Her power was not to destroy, but to enlighten.

Kenshō: seeing the true essence. A glimpse only, a fleeting moment of understanding, the self dropping away to reveal the fundamental nature of things. It required breaking, because a thing without cracks was closed to revelations; that was the purpose of a kōan: to break the usual patterns of thought, opening the mind to new comprehension. And if that mind was ready, then afterward it would be made whole, new gold shining through.

Senzai's mind was ready.

And so was Kazue's.

Chapter Eighteen

The wind still whipped across the mountaintop as fiercely as ever, but the crackling energy of the air was gone.

Senzai stood just an arm's length away from Kazue. Her hair floated and tangled in the breeze, but had returned to its normal length. Her clothing was the sturdy, practical garb Kazue had first seen. And her eyes no longer glowed.

She caught Kazue before she could fall—which might have saved Kazue's life, given the precipitous drop that surrounded her on three sides.

They sank to the ground together. Kazue wondered, with distant, giddy delirium, whether further mastery of the knot tattoo would allow her to use it without this kind of exhaustion afterward. She felt a hundred times more drained than she had after Heidoku, and wasn't sure how much of that was because she had shown Senzai a glimpse of the true essence, how much was because she had glimpsed that true essence herself, and how much was because she'd fought a yōkai and run up a mountain before opening herself to the universe.

She doubted she would have many opportunities to find out. Now that she truly understood the function of her tattoo, she knew that she could use it for its intended purpose—but only with great caution. Not everyone was susceptible to such an epiphany, and of those who were, not all would survive it. Minds like Senzai's were rare. Anyone who was unprepared to receive that moment of ken-shō would almost certainly meet Heidoku's fate.

But even if they did…they weren't gone forever. In the records of the High House of Light she would find the name Togashi Chiaki: the woman she had been in her previous incarnation. Her pursuit of spiritual insight then had led her into enlightened madness, and she spent the last twenty years of her life imprisoned for the safety of both others and herself.

The last twenty years of her life. But not the lives that followed.

"Thank you," Senzai whispered. She released Kazue and crawled backward a small distance, until she could bow to the ground as Kazue had done, earlier that day. "Without you, I would still be lost."

"Please, don't," Kazue said weakly. Her tongue, which had been so eloquent when guided by the tattoo, now felt as clumsy as an arm gone numb. "Without you, *I* would still be lost. Everything you said when you were—before—was true. I let my fear overwhelm me, and was unworthy of this gift. If I had not met you, if you had not been as wise as you are, I might have met the same fate." She managed to command her body well enough to fold herself into a bow of her own.

They both remained there, heads to the ground, until Senzai laughed. "We could stay here all night, fighting to see which of us can be more humble and grateful. But I'm not a monk, and I'm not immune to the cold. Should we go back?"

Kazue groaned as she climbed to her feet. "I *am* a monk, and I would still like to get out of this wind."

She wouldn't have made it down the ridge without Senzai's help. They negotiated it one careful step at a time, because the footing wasn't really wide enough for two women side by side, but if Kazue tried to stand on her own she had a bad feeling she would pitch headfirst either into the trees or over the cliff.

Things became easier once they reached flatter ground. As Senzai's hut came within view, though, Kazue groaned again. "I am so sorry."

In their absence, the building's structural integrity had given way. The roof sagged drunkenly into the gap where she had punched the kobukaiba through the wall. It still stood—more or less—but what shelter it used to offer was significantly reduced, with the wind sweeping through the hole and out the official doorway.

"It was here long before me," Senzai said. "I don't know what hermit built it, but I think it has almost finished serving its purpose."

She led Kazue to the firepit and then lowered her to the ground, unlooping the arm that had supported her on the walk back. "Wait here a moment."

"Yes, sensei," Kazue said reflexively. Senzai paused, but then continued onward to the hut, not saying anything.

When Kazue had asked to be her student, just a few hours before, Senzai had refused. That was the kobukaiba talking, though—or rather, the isolating impulse that had cut her off from society and transformed her into a kobukaiba. Now…

Now Kazue had no idea. Her tattoo hadn't granted her any knowledge of what Senzai had learned in that moment of kenshō; she only knew that it had ended the transformation, returning Senzai to her human self. Which meant the hermit must have decided to end her isolation—but whether that meant accepting students out here in the wilderness or traveling once more to settled lands, she couldn't guess. Even trying made her brain feel tired.

So she watched, with the fixed stare of someone trying not to collapse, as Senzai poked around in the hut, testing its stability. "I think it will stay up for the rest of the night," Senzai said, emerging once more.

"*Think*," Kazue said with a weary laugh.

Senzai bowed in humorous acknowledgment. "It is the best guess this humble one has to offer."

Kazue levered herself up again. "I honestly don't care if it falls on my head. I'm not certain I'll wake up even if it does."

She stopped at the doorway, though, one hand over the gouges the kobukaiba's claws had carved through the wood. "You're taking the futon, though. No arguments."

Senzai bowed again. "As you say."

Kazue slept like lead, except for one dream.

In it she saw Senzai in the doorway again, where she'd stood in her yōkai form when she came hunting Kazue. This time, though, the moonlight haloed a figure that was serene and at peace, rather than wild with power twisted in on itself.

"I wish I could offer you a better blessing," this Senzai murmured. "But your fate is not a simple one, and so I can say only this: that although your power will sometimes bring harm, you must not fear it. The Empire is fast approaching a time when both madness and enlightenment will be needed."

In the dream, those words made sense. But when Kazue awoke, both sense and Senzai were gone.

Chapter Nineteen

Nothing was missing. The cooking pot, the single bowl, Senzai's small collection of tools—they were all still where they'd been the day before. But Kazue felt the difference: the hut was not merely empty now, but uninhabited.

If it weren't for the footprints in the dirt around the fire, she might almost have wondered if the entire thing had been a lengthy dream, or an illusion placed on her by some trickster spirit. But she could see the marks of Senzai's long occupation, and besides, the memory of the previous night was too vivid to be denied. The hermit really had transformed; Kazue really had fought and fled and redeemed her. She had the sore muscles and the sense of inner peace to prove it.

Possibly she was wrong about Senzai having left for good. But she couldn't wait around to find out. However beneficial or even necessary her time in the wilderness had been, Kazue was a samurai, and she had a duty to her lord. A duty she had cast aside for too long already.

She did do one thing before she left, though.

There was a flat-sided stone near the stream where Senzai had knelt to get water. Kazue was just barely strong enough to dig it out from the bank and carry it to the hut, dropping it with the heavy end downward in front of the doorway. Then she took her knife and, heedless of dulling it, scratched a series of characters into the surface:

I could not see how
to untie a knot without
beginning or end—
when I asked the mountain wind,
its answer was simply, *om*.

She bowed before the stone and clapped her hands, offering up a prayer for Senzai, wherever her path took her.

Then she stood and began her own journey home.

Mitsu didn't run. A senior monk should never be seen running for any reason other than physical training or battle. Certainly not in response to a message from one of the novices at the foot of the peak, saying that someone was on their way up the thousand steps.

Because he didn't run, he reached the top of the stairs only a little before Kazue did. But she had her chin down, looking at the weathered stone in front of her rather than the monastery above, and so he had a brief opportunity to study her before she looked up and noticed his presence.

She was thin and dirty, her arms mottled with bruises and scrapes. Her hair had begun to grow out—but only begun; it was clear she had continued to shave her scalp during her absence. That sight gave Mitsu hope.

As did the sight of Kazue at all. Enough time had passed that he'd begun to fear she would never return.

She seemed utterly unsurprised to find him waiting for her. Before Mitsu could say anything, she knelt before him and bowed low. "Senpai. I have come to submit myself for judgment."

All the breath went out of Mitsu. Of course she understood. She'd been a member of the order for too long not to realize that there would be consequences for running away.

And she had come back to face them.

So he didn't say anything to welcome her. He didn't tell her how relieved he was to see her, or ask what had happened while she was gone. He only said, "Follow me."

Kazue rose without another word. He led her to one of the cells used for discipline, where erring monks meditated on their failures. There were no locks: being at the High House of Light was simultaneously inevitable and a choice. Now that she had returned, Kazue's own sense of duty would keep her in that cell.

"I will bring you paper and a brush," he said as she knelt on the stone floor. "You will write out your report and confession, and I will take them to Hassuno-sama."

"Thank you, senpai," Kazue said softly.

Mitsu turned to go. But he couldn't walk away without asking. "Kazue-san—did you find what you needed?"

The barest hint of a smile touched her face. "Yes. I did."

Breathing in a sigh of gratitude, he went to fetch writing materials.

Hassuno-sama sat with Kazue's report spread on the table in front of her. "Mitsu-san," she said. "What do you think of Kazue-san's situation?"

She had allowed him to read the account. It covered everything from Fuchi Mura to Kazue's return to the High House of Light, and as near as Mitsu could tell, she hadn't spared herself in the account. There was no attempt to apologize or justify, only the simple reporting of facts.

Mitsu chose his words carefully. "I think the Heavens guided her. This Senzai, whoever she is, seems to have been precisely the teacher Kazue-san needed."

"Do you think that is how we should view this?" Hassuno-sama tapped the rice paper. "As Kazue-san following her own path?"

His jaw tensed. That was its effect, yes—and he wanted to lean on the effect, using it to spare Kazue the consequences of her actions.

But they had to consider motivation as well as effect. And Mitsu would be failing her as well as the order if he tried to leave that out.

"No, iemoto-sama," he said. "Our teachings encourage us to follow whatever path is necessary...but I do not believe that was what Kazue intended when she left Fuchi Mura. She reacted out of fear, giving in to one of the three sins. Her fear and her regret over what happened to Heidoku caused her to abandon her duty. The fact that doing so led her to where she needed to be does not erase the fact that she surrendered to weakness."

Hassuno-sama regarded him with a steady eye. "There was a time, Mitsu-san, when you would not have admitted that so readily."

He thought of Heidoku, and the struggle he'd felt over the man's crime. "I feel compassion for her, Hassuno-sama. But compassion must be balanced with other concerns, or in the long run, it will create more problems than it solves."

"Indeed." She folded Kazue's report and set it aside. "Then you know what must be done, Mitsu-san. Tell her to come to the Garden of the Elements at dawn tomorrow."

Kazue bathed carefully, dressed herself in a plain white robe, and prayed.

Then she left her cell and, with the measured strides of meditation, went to the Garden of the Elements.

It was one of the masterpieces of the High House of Light. She had not seen it in this lifetime, but it had scarcely changed. The boulders were a little more overgrown with moss, the flowering plants a little taller, the lanterns a little more weathered. The gravel in the dry garden had been raked into a different pattern. A stream wound through it all, crossing beneath her feet three times on her way to the heart of the garden; the arbors over the bridges were, like the gates she had passed through months before, an opportunity to cleanse herself of the three sins.

At the heart of the garden stood a five-tiered stupa. Like the design of the garden itself, it represented the Five Elements: a cube for Earth, a sphere for Water, a pyramid for Fire, a hemisphere for Air, and the lotus flower of the Void on top.

Mitsu and Hassuno-sama waited for her there, unmoving as Kazue knelt before them. He had instructed her the night before, but Kazue had scarcely needed it; she'd been in his position once, lifetimes ago, overseeing someone else's atonement.

She was a monk, but she was also a samurai. She had fled her duty. A bushi or a courtier or even a shugenja might be made rōnin for a failure like hers, but the ise zumi were never put out of the High House of Light like that.

There was another punishment, though. One that expunged a person's shame, so that they would not carry it with them into the next life.

"Kazue-san." Hassuno-sama's voice was serene and cool. "Do you acknowledge your failure?"

"I do, iemoto-sama."

"What explanation do you offer for it?"

"None, iemoto-sama."

"Why do you come here this morning?"

She touched her forehead to the moss. "To ask permission to expunge my shame with suicide."

Hassuno-sama said, "Granted."

Mitsu stepped forward, bearing a small jade cup in his hands. Kneeling with a grace and lightness unexpected in a man his size, he offered it to Kazue with a bow.

The liquid within smelled faintly smoky, as if it carried the scent of a funeral pyre. In the lessons the novices learned, it was called *kiyomizu*: purifying water.

"Drink," Hassuno-sama said. "Die, and be reborn, and return to us cleansed of this shame."

Kazue drank.

Ise zumi were samurai. But when they died, their karma returned them to the High House of Light, through one incarnation after another. Seppuku, the honorable suicide of a bushi or a courtier, would only force the order to go through the long, tedious work of training that soul again.

They had other methods of dealing with such matters.

She saw her life as if from outside: not a sequence of events, as it had been during her gempuku, but a shape laid before her all at once. For an instant she could feel how every piece of it fit together: her flight from Fuchi Mura and her childhood as the daughter of a rōnin mother, the friendships she'd formed in the High House of Light and the animalistic purity of her solitude in the mountains, Senzai and Mitsu, her tattoo and the perilous enlightenment it offered.

Then it faded. One by one the pieces dropped away, dissolving into darkness, until there was nothing left but the Void.

The Void—and herself.

She awoke on the thick moss at the heart of the Garden of the Elements. Golden light flooded the space, the rich warmth of the hour before sunset. The symbolic death bestowed by the purifying water had lasted only a sun's span.

Mitsu helped her sit up. Her body had gone weak again: not as badly as after her gempuku, but enough to make movement uncertain. Whatever was in the kiyomizu, it had a significant effect, not easily shaken off.

"Welcome back," he said, smiling for the first time since her arrival at the top of the stairs.

She tried to respond, and found herself coughing instead. He offered her another cup—ordinary water this time—and when she had finished drinking it, another voice came from behind her. "Mitsu-san. We are not yet finished."

Mitsu nodded in acknowledgment, but slipped her a sidelong wink as he did so. Then he rose and came back a moment later with a small writing desk.

Hassuno-sama might not have moved that entire day. She stood patiently until Mitsu had arranged the paper, ink, and brush. Then she said, "The one who failed has died. You are reborn among us, and so it is time to choose your new name."

Unlike a few months before, this time she had not chosen her name ahead of time. She sat motionless with the brush in her hand for a long moment, her mind an unhelpful blank. She could not be who she had been before—and yet who should she be, if not that woman?

The paradox resonated in her bones. Like being an ise zumi: fated to return to the High House of Light, free in every lifetime to choose that path.

She wet the brush and wrote.

Mitsu's eyebrows rose when he came to take the paper from her. But he said nothing, only bore it to Hassuno-sama, who frowned at the characters written there.

Togashi Kazue.

But instead of "one eternity," this time she had written it with different characters. Now it meant "blessed destiny."

"An unusual choice," Hassuno-sama said at last. "But not, I think, an inappropriate one." She returned the paper to Mitsu. "Welcome to the order, Togashi Kazue-san. May you serve the Dragon Clan well."

Epilogue

This time Mitsu made no requests. He did not even receive a summons. He was simply walking along one of the porticos that looked out over the deep valleys beyond the monastery when he realized he was not alone.

And in the High House of Light, only one man wore full armor.

Mitsu knelt immediately, pressing his forehead to the boards. With anyone else, it might have been a chance encounter. But this was Togashi Yokuni, the clan champion. He did not idly wander the monastery. If he crossed someone's path, it was because he intended to.

The voice came from above, deep and unmuffled by the mempō that covered his face. "You have changed."

One did not argue with one's clan champion. "Yes, Togashi-ue."

"Though still impulsive, you have gained in restraint. Your actions regarding Kazue-san have shown more wisdom than before."

"I have done my best to serve, Togashi-ue."

His only answer was the rush of wind. Minutes passed, and Mitsu strained his ears for the sound of footfalls, wondering if the clan champion had moved on—surely if anyone could move quietly in such armor, it would be him. But Mitsu didn't risk a glance upward. He would kneel here until nightfall if he had to.

He didn't have to.

"Yes. You will serve very well." The tone was thoughtful, detached. "I name you, Togashi Mitsu, as my heir."

Mitsu's whole body jerked. One instinct tried to yank him upright; the other, fortunately stronger, kept him pinned to the boards. "Togashi-ue—"

He'd guessed that he was being measured for some new duty. It had crossed his mind that he might become Hassuno-sama's heir, the inheritor of the order's traditions. That prospect had been difficult enough: not to wander anymore. Not to see the Empire in all its glory and disgrace, offering his aid to those who lacked the power to help themselves. Spending the rest of his life here at the High House of Light.

But this…this was worse. Isolating himself even from his fellow monks. Locking his body into that armor.

For one wild instant, he wished he had made a misstep with Kazue. Shown himself to be too reckless and foolish to ever bear more responsibility than he held right now.

Only for an instant. Because he had done what his conscience and sense of honor demanded…and they would not let him flee from this duty.

The clan champion knew that. He would not have chosen Mitsu were it otherwise.

Mitsu forced himself to subside, repairing his damaged bow. "I am not worthy, Togashi-ue, but I humbly accept."

Words. But given enough time, he could make them true.

He would have to.

"Rise, Mitsu," Togashi Yokuni said. "You have tasks to perform still in the outside world. The first is to find the hermit Kazue-san encountered—the woman called Senzai."

Mitsu climbed to his feet, mystified. Kazue had praised Senzai's wisdom…but surely there were many wise people in the world. "My lord?"

"Yes," he whispered, gazing out across the mountains, into distances Mitsu could only guess at. "Find her—for the sake of the Empire."

About the Author

Marie Brennan is a former anthropologist and folklorist who shamelessly pillages her academic fields for material. She most recently misapplied her professors' hard work to the Hugo Award-nominated Victorian adventure series The Memoirs of Lady Trent; the first book of that series, *A Natural History of Dragons*, was a finalist for the World Fantasy Award and won the Prix Imaginales for Best Translated Novel. *Turning Darkness Into Light*, a stand-alone sequel to the Memoirs, was recently published in the U.S. and U.K. She is also a co-author of the collaborative novel *Born to the Blade* and the author of the Doppelganger duology of *Warrior* and *Witch*, the urban fantasies *Lies and Prophecy* and *Chains and Memory*, the Onyx Court historical fantasy series, the Varekai novellas, and more than fifty short stories. For more information, visit www.swantower.com or her Patreon at https://www.patreon.com/swan_tower.

Rokugan

五輪伝

An Empire in Turmoil

A land where honor is stronger than steel. Here, the samurai of the seven Great Clans serve the Emperor as warriors, courtiers, priests, and monks. They live—and die—by the tenets of Bushidō.

The Dragon Clan has a reputation for being reclusive and mysterious, and none of its people are more enigmatic than the monks of the Togashi Tattooed Order. The ways of this "family" are almost unrecognizable to most samurai, and the powers of their tattoos defy explanation.

The Origins of the Togashi

When the Kami Hantei cut his siblings from the stomach of their father, the depraved Lord Moon, they fell to the Ningen-dō, the Realm of Mortals. One of them, Fu Leng, fell through the earth to Jigoku, the Realm of Evil, and became corrupted. Hantei himself became the first Emperor of Rokugan. The other seven founded the Great Clans of Rokugan, in most cases taking mortal lovers and bearing or siring children to carry on their names.

Togashi-no-Kami was the exception. Reclusive and enigmatic by nature, he joined the others in creating the Empire of Rokugan, but he did not participate in the Tournament of the Kami to choose the first Emperor. And although he founded the Dragon Clan to pursue his ideals of individualism, destiny, and the quest for Enlightenment, he did not found a family. Uniquely among the samurai families of Rokugan, the Togashi of the Dragon Clan are not a family at all—at least, not in the sense of people bound together by heredity.

History remembers the names of Mirumoto and Agasha, two of Togashi's early followers who founded families of their own, but not of the three who dedicated themselves entirely to learning from the Kami. Caught up in his own contemplations, Togashi neither heeded them nor turned them away. The three silently followed him on his travels, always at a respectful distance, and meditated when he did, asking nothing of their sensei save the right to be in his presence.

This continued until the nascent Dragon Clan emerged from the northern mountains and joined the rest of the Empire. On that day, Togashi-no-Kami turned to his three patient students and asked them how long they would follow him. They answered as one, saying, "For the rest of our lives, and all the lives to come."

Togashi-no-Kami laid his hand on each of them in turn, marking their skin with mysterious symbols. Then he turned and pointed at a distant mountain peak. "Build a place for me there," he said, "and I will reward you."

The three set to work right away. To their joy, they discovered the marks had changed them: one had the strength of a hundred, one could work without sleeping, and one could fly like a bird. Together, they labored for an entire year at the top of the mountain. The result was a beautiful monastery: the High House of Light.

Ever since, this remote fastness has been home not only to the Dragon Clan Champions, but to the order that bears Togashi's name. The names of its builders, meanwhile, have been forgotten…and perhaps they were never more than a myth to begin with.

The High House of Light

The High House of Light is a breathtaking sight. It lacks the graceful delicacy of Crane architecture and the monumental grandeur of the Lion, but its presence in the harsh mountains of the North creates a seemingly impossible juxtaposition between human achievement and the untamed splendor of the wilderness. Within its walls, the aesthetic is an austere one: meditation halls with vast expanses of polished wood floor, gardens of raked gravel, and walls of unscalable smoothness.

Although the site could serve as a fortress, it has never been assaulted, nor is it likely to be. More than its isolated location protects it: some spiritual force seems to keep it hidden, so that only invited visitors and those on their way to join the order can even find it. For others, the mountains seem trackless and without end, offering no hint that a community of people lives anywhere nearby.

As a result, the monastery is nearly as legendary as its inhabitants. Most Rokugani hear only tales of its Library of Echoes, staffed by Togashi chroniclers and filled with stories of Rokugan's past; its Garden of the Elements, dedicated to Earth, Water, Air, Fire, and Void; its Plum Blossom Hall, where every day a monk brings a single flower from an everblooming tree and lays it in an alcove in memory of the plum blossom that once fell for Togashi-no-Kami. The average samurai hears these stories and may wonder why it is that so few are permitted to visit and appreciate these marvels.

THE DRAGON'S SON

Although members of the Togashi family are not descended from their founder, it is not quite true to say that Togashi-no-Kami has no descendants.

To most, the unassuming monk named Togashi Hoshi is simply another follower of Togashi who seeks Enlightenment. Yet he is much more than an ise zumi: he is an immortal shapeshifter—and Togashi's son. At times, he serves the monks at the High House of Light, while at other times, he wanders the Empire and the Spirit Realms. By taking different forms, he has kept his true identity secret from even the most scholarly of his order, and even he does not yet know why—for his destiny lies upon its own path.

Joining the Order

The Togashi family is synonymous with the Togashi Order of tattooed monks, or *ise zumi*: a collection of people connected by shared training and oaths. Their origins, however, are much more varied.

No one is born into the family, but neither does the order recruit. Instead, from time to time, a child—or sometimes even an adult—feels a sudden conviction that it is their destiny to go to the High House of Light. Many of these individuals are members of the Dragon Clan, but the call knows no borders; people from as far away as Crab Clan lands or the Islands of Spice and Silk have been known to journey into the mountains that conceal the monastery.

Nor are they all samurai. Although the ise zumi—uncommonly among monks—belong to that class, those who seek to join them may be samurai, rōnin, or peasants; some rumors even claim hinin, the caste at the bottom of the Celestial Order, have joined the ranks of the tattooed monks. No one questions a person when they arrive at the monastery: if they have succeeded in finding it, they clearly belong there.

Sometimes it happens that aggrieved parents try to bar their child from going. This meets with little success. Those who are called will ask for the blessings of their family and lord, but if those are withheld, they may run away—years later, if need be. Those who feel the call inevitably find a way—perhaps only in their next life.

NOVITIATE

The training of the ise zumi is an odd hybrid of samurai and monastic education. Like monks of the Brotherhood of Shinsei, tattooed monks study theology extensively. Togashi-no-Kami was visited by Shinsei, the Little Teacher, after the Day of Thunder. According to legend, when Shinsei asked Togashi why he isolated himself in the mountains, Togashi explained that he would not move from his meditation until he understood. To this, Shinsei responded, "Neither will I." For the nine days of their meditation together, Shinsei refused to eat or drink or move from where he sat. On the tenth day, when Shinsei was near death, Togashi finally understood that his quest for wisdom had affected the world around him. A plum blossom fell into his lap, and he was enlightened.

But the theology of the ise zumi does not focus solely on the Tao of Shinsei. The ise zumi also study the Great Fortunes and the countless Lesser Fortunes upon whom the religion of the Empire centered in the days before the Kami. In addition, they study the Spirit Realms, the Kami who founded the Great Clans, the mikokami that make up the physical world, and the honored ancestors.

They also practice *jūjutsu*. True mastery of the elements requires one to develop the body as well as the soul. Even those who do not expect ever to engage in a real fight often develop great skill in unarmed combat through training. A few undertake the study of weapons as well. Further, like their Brotherhood counterparts, ise zumi seek to master the "inner teachings" of kihō, which allow them to stretch their capabilities beyond ordinary human limits. An ise zumi may be able to see with an eagle's clarity, feel the tremors of faraway footsteps, or even heat their body to searing temperatures.

But unlike ordinary monks, ise zumi also learn the history and etiquette of samurai society—including the virtues of Bushidō. They see much less division between the latter and the ethics of monastic life than their colleagues in the Brotherhood do, and while they do not devote as much energy and zeal to protecting their honor as the average Lion or Crane might, insulting an ise zumi can still be a dangerous risk to take.

The years of novitiate serve additional purposes: to erode the divisions that separate the trainees and give them new identities as members of the Togashi family. A novice of samurai origins who thinks this makes them superior to their peasant-born sibling soon finds themself broken of that notion, and a former Matsu and a former Kakita will be made to cooperate in training exercises until the rivalry of their former families ceases to mean anything to them.

Life at the High House of Light is harsh and simple. Novices carry out the vast majority of the work performed by heimin servants at other dōjō, from sweeping the paths to cooking meals to washing laundry. Even full monks are quite willing to perform humble tasks when necessary, if there is no novice around to take care of them.

But for all the strict discipline of monastic life, ise zumi enjoy certain elements of freedom. Even as novices, they are permitted and encouraged to pursue hobbies: the study of history; creation of ink wash paintings; mastery of the bow; or practice of any other scholarly, artistic, or martial skill that calls to them. There is wisdom in everything, and tattooed monks are encouraged to seek that wisdom wherever they can.

GEMPUKU

Although few outsiders are aware of it, when ise zumi finish their novitiate and become adults, they undergo a gempuku rite of passage designed to test their mastery of the skills they have studied.

For would-be tattooed monks, this test takes place in three stages. The first measures their skill in jūjutsu by requiring them to fight against the senior jūjutsu sensei or other master of the form. This is not a duel, with the novice failing if they lose; expecting a student to defeat an experienced monk would be profoundly unfair. Instead, the sensei's goal is to evaluate the novice's skills, making certain they have no serious weaknesses of form, strength, or tactical reasoning.

Once this first trial ends, the novice moves on to the scholarly examination. Three sensei oversee this, spending hours questioning the candidate on matters of theology. Brute strength without wisdom and understanding of the world would do the order no good; here again, the evaluators' purpose is to expose any shortcomings, any areas of ignorance that mean the novice is not yet ready to join the ranks of the full monks. Coming on the heels of the jūjutsu match, this examination also tests the candidate's endurance and concentration.

If the student passes both of these trials, they retire to a secluded chamber with a single sensei, who places a candle in front of them and guides them through a new form of meditation. Repeating the question "What do you remember?" the sensei leads the candidate back through the memories of their current lifetime…and, if they are truly ready, into memories of the lives that came before.

This, many say, is the true gempuku, and the first two trials are merely pageants. An ise zumi is one who knows the truth of themself and their past. Without that, skill at jūjutsu and knowledge of theology are nothing. Only once a monk completes their gempuku are they worthy to receive their first tattoo.

"And All the Lives to Come"

The pledge made by the founders of the ise zumi order was no mere boasting. It was a promise, and one that every tattooed monk after them has upheld.

Once an ise zumi, always an ise zumi. Regardless of where their karma takes them in the next life—to the lands of another clan, to humble or exalted birth—every member of the Togashi Order eventually returns. This is the source of the call felt by those who seek the High House of Light; they subconsciously remember their pledge, and they return to the monastery to take up their service once more.

The scholars of the order's history say this cycle is intimately linked to their tattoos. The power of these marks is not easily mastered; without the proper preparation, the risk to one's physical and spiritual well-being is too great. Finding balance with these energies and channeling them to their purpose requires not just years but entire lifetimes of training. Great masters like Togashi Mitsu are the product of centuries of effort.

Any given monk does not remember all of their previous lives, of course. Passage through Meido washes souls clean of their memories; in most cases, only fragments remain. But the training of an ise zumi teaches them to access those fragments, drawing on them to broaden their understanding of proper action and to use their tattoos effectively. In some cases, the tattoos they receive in a particular lifetime are a response to the previous one, expanding on the lessons of karma or unlocking deeper secrets.

Odd little echoes can linger as well. The peculiar hobbies some ise zumi take up, even during their novice years, are often remnants of some earlier incarnation's activity. It is rare for a monk to be able to call on such skills directly, manifesting great ability without new training, but on occasion it happens, especially in times of profound need.

The karmic destiny of ise zumi is one of the order's most well-kept secrets. Even the leaders of the other Dragon families are not aware that the ise zumi return to the order repeatedly through many lifetimes. Any ise zumi who completes their gempuku and remembers this truth is deeply unlikely to share it with an outsider—after all, they have protected that secret before.

The Hierarchy of the Ise Zumi

Compared with the elaborate ranks of the armies of bushi or the bureaucracies of courtiers, the hierarchy of the ise zumi seems nearly nonexistent. Once novices become full monks, there are relatively few titles or positions of authority they can aspire to—nor are they expected to do so, as desire, along with fear and regret, is one of the fundamental three sins of the cosmos.

Almost every notable position within the order can be classified under the title of sensei, or teacher. There are teachers for jūjutsu, for meditation, for calligraphy, and for the different branches of theology. Unlike the -*sama* honorific given to lords elsewhere in the Empire, -*sensei* simply marks a person as "one who was born before another," acknowledging that person's seniority and greater experience. Seniority is the main source of authority at the High House of Light, whether among novices or full monks—though its force is complicated by the recollection of previous lives, such that a younger monk like Togashi Mitsu may be acknowledged as senior by virtue of their accumulated experience. This hidden variable often confuses outsiders.

Other positions are born of logistical necessity. A neglected library will soon see its precious scrolls lost to mold and insects, so the Togashi chroniclers and their assistants are kept busy airing, copying, and adding to the monastery's collections. There are monks in charge of the kitchens, of monastery upkeep, and of procurement of supplies from elsewhere in Dragon Clan lands. They, too, are addressed as sensei; after all, their experience in such practical matters is vital to keeping the High House of Light functioning. Finally, a very few—such as the ise zumi tasked with serving the Clan Champion and the *iemoto*, or head of the order—have authority of a more conventional variety, such as most samurai would recognize.

Dealing with Dishonor

When ise zumi err, the initial response has more in common with Brotherhood discipline than with the punishments of samurai. Small infractions call for fasting, penitent labor, and meditation on one's mistakes. Novices may be beaten, but this is seen as toughening them as much as inflicting pain for the sake of justice; full monks rarely face physical punishment. Penalties such as fines and demotions mean little to monks who possess almost nothing and have very little hierarchy within their ranks. When it comes to serious matters of dishonor, the Togashi face a peculiar challenge. Given the order's many secrets, they are deeply reluctant to make a member rōnin, lest the outcast spill such matters to the outside world. And both the dishonor of execution and the more honorable end of seppuku serve very little purpose, except to put the order's sensei through the work of training that person all over again in their next lifetime.

For those offenders, there are alternatives. A form of symbolic suicide, drinking a medicine called *kiyomizu*, or "purifying water," takes the place of seppuku and allows the repentant monk to be spiritually reborn, washed clean of their failings. An unrepentant monk, by contrast, might be imprisoned for life, with others tasked to reeducate them so they will not carry their mistakes into the next incarnation. Far, far rarer is the penalty of true exile, which has only been carried out a few times in the order's history. This severs the offender from their school, family, and clan far more thoroughly than mere rōnin status: it strips them of their tattoos, leaving their skin scarred and bare, and breaks the karmic chain that would lead them back to the order after reincarnation. Such people are no longer ise zumi, in this life or in any of the lives to come.

Naimyō and Gaimyō

A strange dichotomy runs through the Togashi Order. Many of its members enter the High House of Light for training and never leave again, renouncing the wider world of the Empire. Others journey extensively through the lands of other clans for a variety of purposes. Among the ise zumi, these are known as *naimyō* and *gaimyō* respectively: inside and outside lives.

The reasons for this division lie in the peculiar nature of the Tattooed Order. The character used to write "life" in those two words specifically refers to a person's mortal existence: a lifetime, a step along the path of reincarnation. Any given ise zumi generally spends several lives as a naimyō, then one as a gaimyō, then returns to the High House of Light for another span. This gives them the opportunity to hone their power before employing it in the world. Outsiders may wonder why the Dragon Clan puts so much effort into training people to master skills they never use for practical ends, but tattooed monks think on a much longer time scale: skills practiced in this lifetime can find their purpose in the next.

Such thinking also ties into ise zumi philosophy regarding the balance between contemplation and action. Much like a duelist of the Kakita takes pride in their ability to center themself and then defeat their opponent with a single perfect strike, an ise zumi learns to study the world around them and find the single point at which they can intervene to change events. If that point does not come in this lifetime…there is always another one after it.

Asceticism

The concept of monasticism is almost inextricably intertwined with asceticism, and in this respect, the Togashi are not much different from Brotherhood monks. Within the High House of Light, food is simple and served in moderation—though a courtier or shugenja would be astonished by the "moderate" quantities required to support the physical labor and martial training of ise zumi. All but the most senior monks sleep in communal dormitory rooms and maintain a rigorous schedule of training, meditation, and labor.

But the true meaning of asceticism is not poverty or denial: it is non-attachment. Most monks own very few personal possessions, and more importantly, they do not desire more.

A HIDDEN DESTINY

Outsiders wonder why ise zumi practice many martial techniques and other skills, yet live out their lives atop a mountain where those skills never see practical use. The ise zumi know the answer but have an unanswered question of their own: Why does the order exist at all?

They understand that in some lives they are gaimyō and that, in those cases, their tattoos and abilities may make a difference in the world. But why did Togashi-no-Ka-mi choose to imbue some of his followers with a power so complex and difficult it takes lifetimes to master? Why bind them to rein-carnate into the order, instead of allowing them to drift from fate to fate as other souls do?

No ordinary monk knows the answer to that question. Possibly the head of the order, does—but it is equally possible that the only person living who can say for cer-tain is the Dragon Clan Cham-pion. Regardless, more than a few ise zumi have considered this question and, in light of their founder's foresight, reached a chilling conclusion: that Togashi-no-Kami had a vision of some future moment in which their unique pow-ers would be needed.

This thought generally does not frighten them. The ise zumi have dedicated countless lives to the order; most are eager for the moment when they will be called upon to act. If anything troubles them, it is the question of what will happen *after* that: what will become of the ise zumi when their original purpose is achieved?

If an ise zumi goes out into the world and attends a courtier's lavish banquet, they will not refuse the rich food, but they will eat in moderation and refrain from making a habit of such behavior. If a high-ranking samurai offers them a gift in gratitude for their assistance, they need not give offense by refusing it—but later, if they find someone in need of that item, they will give it away without hesitation.

Ise zumi almost never marry. For the samurai of Rokugan, the main purpose of marriage is the continuation of the family or the forging of political alliance. Given that the Togashi family perpetuates itself by other means, children are unnec-essary, and the Togashi's reclusive tendencies means they make poor material for politics. On rare occasions, however, ise zumi have sired or borne children, usually to achieve some greater purpose—sometimes political, but often more mysterious than that.

Apparent diversions from asceticism can be a point of great contention within the order. In the end, only an individual monk can be certain whether they engage in sensory pleasures without becoming attached to them, or whether their assertion of nonattachment is mere justification for indulgence. Those who are truly strong in spirit can appreciate the transient joy of such things and then release it without any lingering regret. But they are few in number, and many fewer than sometimes claim that status. In the end, it is easier to abstain than to test one's will—although that can be a mark of fear, which, like desire and regret, is one of the three sins. So the debates continue, and they are unlikely to ever end.

Ise Zumi Tattoos

The images inked into the skin of Togashi monks are famous even in the farthest reaches of the Empire. People who have never met an ise zumi still recognize the concept of a "tattooed monk": they are stock figures in popular entertainment, with actors painting artwork onto their bodies. Unscrupulous bandits and other criminals have been known to frighten the credulous with their own ordinary tattoos, claiming those hold great power.

Although Togashi monks sometimes get ordinary tattoos for decorative purposes, all of their spiritual marks are inked by the order's tattoo master. The first two of these are awarded at the end of the gempuku and, in a way, can be seen as a fourth trial: despite

all their training in this lifetime and the ones before it, not everyone can withstand the energy that floods their bodies. Most fall unconscious for at least a day, and some wind up with their health permanently damaged.

While all full monks have at least two tattoos, more senior members of the order often have more. In fact, the number of tattoos a monk possesses is itself a kind of seniority. Age and time in the order also play a role in establishing seniority, but since the masters and sensei may grant additional tattoos as a form of reward or increased responsibility, the less unmarked skin a monk has, the more respect they earn. Most tattoos take the form of natural phenomena, such as animals, flowers, trees, clouds, or other such symbols. Abstract designs are less common, and often signal more unusual effects. Only rarely does a tattoo depict a human-made object like a torii gate or a folding fan.

The ise zumi maintain extensive records of tattoo images and their effects to aid new monks in identifying the purpose of their tattoos. Many common marks take more or less the same form and have had the same effect throughout the centuries; still, a known effect can show up with a different image, and a familiar image can have an unfamiliar effect. Dragon samurai who are not ise zumi often get ordinary tattoos as a sign of solidarity with their more mysterious brethren.

When the purpose of a tattoo is not well-known, it can take a monk quite some time to work out how to use it. A few come out of their tattooing with an instinctive understanding of a mark's power, but most have to engage in meditation and experimentation before they

THE SECRET OF THE TATTOOS

Even among the ise zumi, very few know the source of their tattoos' power. Customarily, this secret belongs only to the clan champion; the clan champion's heir; the *iemoto*, or head of the order; and the current tattoo master. To share it more widely could be devastating, because to an outsider's eye, it looks a great deal like *mahō*: the blood magic granted by *kansen*, the elemental kami corrupted by the power of Jigoku, the Realm of Evil.

Like the power of mahō, the power of the tattoos arises from blood. However, in the case of the tattoos, the blood is that of Togashi-no-Kami himself, contained in a *nemuranai* vial that never runs dry. Mixed into ink, it imbues tattooed images with supernatural force. This has no connection to the kansen that seek to sway mortals with Jigoku's influence—but the ise zumi have no desire to explain that to Kuni Witch Hunters, Asako Inquisitors, or the Scorpion Clan's Black Watch. Because of this, the source of the tattoos' power is withheld even from most members of the order.

grasp it. Experimentation may also help a monk learn to use a tattoo in additional ways, strengthening or decreasing its effects or applying those effects in unusual circumstances.

Although the effects of the tattoos often resemble those of kihō, the spiritual techniques commonly developed by monks, the Togashi tattoos differ in their degree of potency and in that they must be uncovered or lightly covered in order to work. Ise zumi do not wear light clothing and simple fabrics for purely ascetic reasons or simply to show off the beauty of their decorations; it is necessary for them to unleash their full power. Much of the hardship they endure as novices is intended to strengthen their bodies so they will not need armor or warm. heavy clothing to protect themselves, which would interfere with their tattoos.

Enlightened Madness

Deep in the records of the order, in scrolls only a select few are permitted to read, there are tales that explain why the ise zumi must work for lifetimes to master their tattoos. These tales relate what happens when an unprepared spirit is subjected to the divine energies of the ink. This condition is known as "enlightened madness."

The quest for Enlightenment, which frees the soul from the endless cycle of reincarnation, is a major preoccupation of many Dragon samurai, who each seek their own path to that end. But just as there are many roads to Enlightenment, so too are there many roads to enlightened madness. Although it can be found in any corner of the Empire, it is more common among the Dragon, and most common of all among the ise zumi. Still, it is extremely rare, with fewer than one case being reported each generation.

At its heart, it is an affliction caused by glimpsing the truth of reality; instead of being strengthened by the experience, the sufferer's soul and mind shatter. What outward effect this has varies from person to person. Each becomes obsessed with the conviction that they alone understand the true interrelatedness of things, the essential meaninglessness of physical existence, or both. Some turn catatonic, but most begin taking actions that seem inexplicable. When these actions are trivial and empty, they do no one harm, but a person afflicted by enlightened madness is just as likely to commit heinous crimes in their attempt to convince those around them that none of it matters, or to bring about some cosmic end only they can see.

The cruelest part is that the afflicted are not without wisdom. They are not "mad" in an ordinary sense, but driven by half-understood truths. Unfortunately, the half they fail to understand means they may wind up doing more harm than good.